She stuck the book back in her shelf. Then she ran to her bed and buried her head under her pillow, pulling up the covers around her neck.

Knavehearts, yeesh. That brought back some traumatizing memories. Knaves were the most vengeful of all the vampire families. In the Old World, they'd kept an iron claw over land and castles, and they'd fight any hybrid claiming even minimal vampire power. In the end, it was better to be mortal in the New World, her family had decided, than fight pureblood Knaves for all eternity in the Old.

Now one was here, on the search for an heir. Maddy hoped the Knave would just hurry up, find that stupid Tenth, and hightail it back to the Old World, chop chop.

Until then, they were all in danger. Hybrids, rats, humans—everyone.

THE KNAVEHEART'S CURSE

A
VAMPIRE ISLAND
STORY

ADELE GRIFFIN

SCHOLASTIC INC.

New York Toronto London Auckland
Sydney Mexico City New Delhi Hong Kong

ISBN: 978-0-545-22393-5

12 11 10 9 8 7 6 5 4 3 2 1   10 11 12 13 14 15/0

Printed in the U.S.A.   40

First Scholastic printing, January 2010

For Harry and Faye

1

PRESTO!

Sometimes Maddy wished she had more friends. Or even one. She knew she was different from other kids. As a vegetarian fruit-bat vampire, she had roamed the earth for centuries. She had witnessed floods, plagues, wars, and bloody beheadings. Then a few years ago, her family had left the Old World behind, exchanging immortality to live in New York City as ordinary people.

Ordinary-*ish*. On the outside, Maddy looked like your average almost-seventh-grader, but on the inside . . .

"Most eleven-year-olds don't have four-hundred-year-old hearts," she answered herself with a spin of her straw umbrella. Strange, but true. As a vampire, she'd flown around the Old World for many centuries. In New York City, she'd finally turned into a girl—with only a few left-over vampire desires to contend with.

Like capes. It was Saturday morning, and Maddy was on her way to see Carlyle Blake, Tailor Extraordinaire. She needed a real, all-purpose vampire cape. Her last cape had been a purple silk scarf from her Six Wicked Tricks magician kit. Which had worked okay, until Maddy left it out in the rain overnight. By the next morning, it had shrunk to the size of a washcloth.

1

Luckily, Maddy's older sister, Lexington, had seen Carlyle's sign. Since Lex was a word-loving nerd, she knew that *extraordinaire* was a stylish word for "expensive."

"And you're broke," reminded Lexie.

Maddy smirked. She had a secret payment plan.

On this sweaty Saturday, the other kids in Maddy's class were at Smoothie Moo's ice-cream parlor to celebrate Dakota Underhill's birthday party. Everyone (except for Maddy) had been invited. Even crybaby Oliver Watson. Even Ann LeFrack, who picked her scabs and ate them. Dakota was as sweet as a Moo's rainbow-frosted ice-cream cake. Everyone thought Dakota was cool because she had moved here midyear from Queensland, Australia, and she spoke with a twangy Australian accent.

"Dakooty Giampuketro thinks she's so great, but she's not," Maddy muttered as she rang the tailor's buzzer. "Who cares about her stupid party?"

"Shoo, elf. I'm not interested in purchasing Elf Scout cookies." Carlyle Blake had instantly appeared in his door frame to stare down his long nose at Maddy, who was not very tall.

"My name is Madison Livingston, and I'm not an elf or an Elf Scout," she said. "I want a cape."

Before Carlyle could say, "Do come in," she hopped inside. Even with her umbrella and two coats of SXP sunblock—which you can't even get in drugstores without a prescription—the sunshine was harsh on Maddy's paper-thin skin. And the last thing she needed was skin crumbles.

"Do come in," said Carlyle, but by this time Maddy had already leaped up the flight of stairs and into a room of splendid fabrics.

"Ooh. Pretty." Maddy trailed her fingers along the bolts of cloth, but Carlyle, huffing up the steps behind her, stopped her with a slap on the hand.

"How will you pay for this cape?" he asked. "My prices are staggering."

"Presto." And Maddy pulled out her secret payment plan—a triple-strand, black beaded necklace. This past winter, Maddy had inherited the necklace, along with the splendid townhouse where the Livingstones now lived, when she slayed the evil fullblood vampires Nigel and Nicola von Krik. That had been such an awesome day. Too bad the necklace gave Maddy the creeps. Probably because it reminded her too much of the von Kriks.

"Ahh." Carlyle seemed enchanted. He scooped it up and held it to the window, where it sparkled and twinkled. Then dropped it back in Maddy's palm. "Very well. One cape for that necklace."

"Deal." Maddy knew the necklace was worth money, but if she could get it off her hands for a cape, that was an excellent trade.

The tailor measured Maddy's height and shoulder span before letting her pick out fabrics. Maddy chose violet velvet for the outside, with a buttery gold silk lining. "An excellent choice for an opera cape," Carlyle said. "Are you a fan?"

In answer, Maddy burst into the Queen of the Night's

aria from *The Magic Flute* as she'd first heard it a couple of hundred years ago, hanging upside down in bat form from the rafters of the State Opera House. All vampires love opera and the juicy, plump performers who sing it.

Some people, however, did not like Maddy's opera voice. Carlyle was holding his ears. "Enough. Leave me your phone number and I'll call you when your cape is ready. In the meantime, no surprise visits."

On the way home, Maddy decided to take a quick detour to Moo's. Not because she cared about Dakota's cake and presents or because she was thinking of interrupting Dakota's party with some of the special pranks she was known for.

No, what she really craved was a cup of strawberry topping. Fruit toppings were the only treat that Maddy, Lexie, and their younger brother, Hudson, could order from ice-cream parlors, because the Livingstones, like most hybrid vampires, followed a mostly fruits-and-veggies diet.

Outside Smoothie Moo's, Maddy peered through the window glass. Inside, it was crowded with her P.S. 42 classmates. Dakota was sitting high up on the Moo Cow patchwork birthday chair. As soon as she saw Maddy, she scrunched down.

Poor thing. Maddy felt kind of bad, figuring Dakooty was remembering some of those lunch swap tricks. Dakota was an easy target, always hoping to trade her food for something sweeter. Like one time, when Maddy had swapped Dakota's white peach for a smelly dish sponge spread thick with cafeteria mayonnaise. "It's vanilla-frosted sponge cake," Maddy'd explained as everyone cringed to watch Dakota bite into chewy, mayonnaise-coated sponge.

Another swap had been Dakota's bunch of grapes in exchange for Maddy's killer garlic-and-white-chocolate-chunk cookies. The lumps of garlic looked like macadamia nuts. Maddy had a special affection for the recipe ever since she'd used it to poison the von Kriks. Since then, she occasionally whipped up batches, hoping she might "accidentally" poison another evil fullblood. So far, no luck. Most humans kept their distance from garlic-flavored cookies, and fullbloods had grown wise to Maddy's tricks.

But Maddy's classmates loved those lunch pranks. Or at least they laughed at them. And Dakota was a pretty good sport. So why was Maddy the only one snubbed and uninvited to Dakota's party?

Maybe if she wished Dakota happy birthday and showed she wasn't planning anything sneaky, they could start fresh.

By now, Dakota's mom, Nora, had spied Maddy. She opened the door. "Come out of the sun, Madison," she said. "Your straw brolly is divine. May I cut you a slice of ice-cream cake?"

Dakota had dropped her spoon. Her bottomless dark eyes widened.

"Just a cup of strawberry topping, thanks," said Maddy.

"Dakota's opening some presents, and then afterward, we're going to do a sing-along on the karaoke."

Karaoke? Yes! Maddy loved to sing. When Dakota gave Maddy a half smile, that did it. Maddy settled into a chair with her cup of topping to watch the rest of the gift-opening. She hoped *The Magic Flute* was on the karaoke menu. Then she would sing out her best mezzo-soprano and dazzle everyone.

"Ooh." Dakota held up a packet. "Monogrammed golf shoes—thanks, Lisi!"

Maybe it's okay that I'm here, Maddy thought. She cleared her throat a couple of times, preparing her voice. Possibly her invitation got lost in the mail, and she was meant to be here all along.

Anyway, now Dakooty, and everyone else, could see that she was the perfect, proper birthday guest.

"So, Maddy, what's up with not bringing a present?" Lisi Elcris was not only Dakota's best friend, but also her beanpole opposite. Her family owned the Elcris Shoe Emporium, which Lisi seemed to think was as important as owning an entire country. She was one of the only kids in school who dared to stand up to Maddy. She was standing up now, her beady eyes hard.

"I forgot," Maddy mumbled.

"If you couldn't afford to buy a real present, you should give a homemade gift." Lisi was speaking too loud. "Any gift. Especially since you're not even supposed to be here."

Maddy slurped another strawberry. Centuries change, she thought, but loudmouths never do.

Other kids had gone quiet, waiting for Maddy to do

something naughty. In truth, Maddy couldn't think of any better trick than decorating Dakota's birthday cake with the dead cricket she'd picked off her front steps this morning that was squished in the bottom of her shorts pocket. In the moment, it now seemed too gross.

"Otherwise, nobody wants you," Lisi insisted. "Right, D.?"

"Right, D.?" aped Lisi's little brother, Adam, who was a couple of grades younger and built like a freckled bowling ball.

"I don't mind." But Dakota looked doubtful.

Maddy sniffed. What was that scent in the air? Grassy, with a hint of sea breeze. Interesting. Maddy's extra-sharp nose honed in. The scent was coming from one of Dakota's birthday gifts.

That one.

Oblong, wrapped in layers of faded tissue paper and twisted with scraggly twine. Something incredible was in that package. Maddy's fingernails itched for it.

"My super-fantastic cousin is visiting us from Denmark. She can do one-hand handsprings." Lisi was still talking in her know-it-all voice. "*That's* a good trick. What can *you* do, Maddy? Besides imitate a shrimp?"

Okay, that was the last straw. Maddy hated to be teased about her height, and she'd already been called an elf today. She pounced, sweeping the gift off the table.

"Presto!" she said, shoving it under her arm. "Witness my spectacular magic trick!"

"What is it?" Kids looked around, confused.

7

"I'm going to make Dakooty's present disappear! Later, blisters!" And with a final hiss for Lisi, Maddy sprang out Moo's door and took off running down the street.

If she couldn't be the perfect party guest, at least she'd found herself a consolation prize.

2

MYSTERY GIFT

Before the Livingstones moved into their townhouse, Maddy had been forced to share a bedroom with her sister. Awful. Lexie and Maddy did not see eye to eye on decorating.

For example, flowers. Gentle Lexie liked them to be kept alive, blooming in vases of water. Not hanging upside down in crunchy bunches. Also, smells. Maddy preferred the odors of sweaty socks and wet sawdust. Unfortunately, Lexie loved sugary breezes of lavender, nutmeg, ginger, and tuberose. Once she'd even set out a bowl of potpourri, which Maddy had mistaken for a snack of sun-dried bugs, an Old World vampire treat.

"Ew, why would anyone display a dish of dead insects?" Lexie shook her head as Maddy hopped around the room, spitting petals.

Thankfully, Maddy was no longer sharing space with Lex. In her hideaway attic bedroom, Maddy could enjoy her own style—dark and damp. To achieve the right mold factor, Maddy had set one humidifier in each corner. After six months, her room was now exquisitely clammy, with mildew like a mat on her floor, while her walls were creeping with constellations of fungus.

Best of all, in the back of Maddy's closet, a dainty colony of toadstools had sprouted through the wood floor cracks.

Maddy inhaled their musty scent as she sat down on her bed, kicking off her sneakers to examine her blisters. She'd walked a lot today. Any human would have been running for a Band-Aid, but hybrid-vampire blood is different, a greenish blue powder that congeals to a crust. Maddy touched the spongy skin bubbles. Good, crusting already.

"Who gave you that present?"

Maddy squeaked. She hadn't seen her younger brother, Hudson, roosting under the eaves. Hudson was the only member of the family who could turn into a bat. This gift—along with being incredibly handsome, plus fluent in animal languages—made Hudson show-offish.

"Susanality," Maddy lied. Susanality was Maddy's best friend. Lexie had a best friend, Pete Stubbe, who was a werewolf, and Hudson had a best human friend, Duane Rigby, and they were always yakking about them at the dinner table.

A few months ago, fed-up Maddy had invented a best friend, Susanality, so that she could have her own turn talking.

"That wrapping paper smells nice. Looks recycled, too," Hudson said approvingly as he stretched his wings and yawned, then spiraled himself into a backflip to land on Maddy's shoulder. "What is it?"

"A friendship present." Maddy shrugged. "Since I'm her best friend and she's my best friend."

"So open it."

Maddy didn't need to be told twice. She untied the tissue. The object was hollow like a pipe, waist high, and smelled like secrets.

Maddy opened the card and read the smudged ink:

For my darling niece, Dakota—
Call on your dearest loud and clear,
Near and far,
When you most need them to come through.
Love,
Your favorite uncle, Godfry

Maddy crumpled the card in her hand before her brother could see.

"What is it?" asked Hudson.

"It's a . . . a walking cane that Susanality made for me."

"What do those initials, G.D.U., stand for?"

"They stand for 'Grrr—Don't Use.'" Maddy knew they stood for Dakota's initials, Gertrude Dakota Underhill, but she was a good on-the-spot liar. And now she wanted to be alone with her gift. "Crud, you know the rules—no roosting in my room without permission. Out!"

She shook him off so that he collided into a very wet and joyful Lexie. Squealing, Hudson dug his hind claws onto his other sister's shoulder as Lex plopped into Maddy's desk chair and clicked the back of her throat.

"What's up?" Her big sister looked so happy that Maddy didn't have the heart to remind her about room rules.

11

"You know that bulletin board at Candlewick Café—the one with all the Help Wanteds? Like for babysitters or Italian lessons?" Lexie paused to breathe as the others nodded. "Well, last week, I saw one that offered to teach guitar accompaniment to all the saddest songs by your favorite doomed artists. So of course I tore off and called the number, and Zelda—that's the name of the teacher—told me the price for lessons. It was way too much money, but fortunately—*ulp!*" Lexie started hiccuping with excitement.

"Fortunately, what?" They were both waiting.

Lexie scooped in a long breath. "Zelda asked why I wanted to learn guitar and I said because I loved sad songs and then I started reciting 'Annabel Lee' and by the sixth stanza—*ulp!*" Lexie hiccuped again. Hudson thwopped her on the back.

"Sixth stanza, what?"

"Zelda said she'd teach me for free! All I'd have to do is help her set up her concerts. She plays at lots of kids' theaters and festiv—Mads, why're you looking at me like I'm chewing gum stuck to your shoe?"

Maddy couldn't help but frown. "Don't get me wrong, you're a great reciter, Lex, but you didn't exactly inherit Mom and Dad's gift for music." Their parents, dog walkers by day, were also members of an alternative rock band called the Dead Ringers. "When you play clarinet, it sounds like a seagull with pneumonia."

"Mom and Dad say I just haven't found my kindred instrument. Maybe it's guitar." Lexie looked thoughtful.

"And Zelda rocks. I met her yesterday in person, and she loves doomed poetry. We're like two long-lost identical twin sisters."

Maddy cut her eyes at Hudson, who wrinkled his nose back at her. Lexie was always hoping to find herself a long-lost identical twin. Maddy and Hudson thought it seemed creepy. Who wanted to run into somebody wearing your face?

Anyway, Lexie and Maddy looked as alike as plenty of sister pairs. Both of them had pencil-straight, ink black hair, matching dark eyes, and ears and noses that pinched slightly on the ends. The main difference was that Lexie was tall and Maddy was not, as if Lexie had somehow stolen Maddy's extra inches for herself.

"If you stink at guitar, we'll tell you," promised Hudson. "Mom and Dad are too easy on you, probably since they can't believe they made a kid who's so tone-deaf. But we don't want anyone to tease you about it—outside of us, that is."

"I hope I have *some* talent." Lexie sighed. "If not, as good ole E. A. Poe would say, 'Oh, my sear'd and blighted heart!'" Lexie's brain was like a weepy accordion file, packed with scraps of sad poems.

"Speaking of seared and blighted, check out my blisters." Maddy stuck out her feet and wriggled. The blobs had just about crusted over.

The others hissed in sympathy. As hybrids turn human, their bodies put a lot of effort into making blood, so they hate to give up even one drop. "As Susanality would say,

'A throbbing toe pain'll drive ye insane.'" When Maddy had invented Susanality, she'd decided that her imaginary friend should possess the Livingstone family flair for quotes, poems, recipes, jigsaw puzzles, geography, history, and dressing up.

But now Lexie had noticed Dakota's gift. "What's that?"

"My new walking cane."

"From Susanality," added Hudson.

"A cane? Why?" asked Lexie. "Do you hobble?"

"Are you hunchbacked?" asked Hudson. They started to laugh.

Maddy jumped up and turned her stick into a weapon. Lexie was easy to prod out the door, but since Hudson could fly, he was trickier. Eventually Maddy had to find her bath towel to snap him off. "Ack, your towel smells like mildew! How can you even use—" But by then Maddy had thrown him out.

Little brothers were so annoying, especially when they could fly.

3

A VISITOR

Maddy waited for sundown to test her cane. She liked the clonk of the wood on the sidewalk cement. She wondered what Dakota's favorite uncle Godfry had meant about calling on friends near and far. Could this stick have powers? Maddy's extra-sensitized vampire fingertips couldn't feel the tingle of a charm or a spell surging through the wood grain.

No sooner had she returned home than the doorbell rang. Maddy hid her gift in the back of the umbrella stand before opening the door. A good thing, too.

There, on the welcome mat, stood the birthday girl herself.

"G'day, Dakooty," said Maddy in her best fake Australian accent.

"I'm only here because you nicked one of my presents." Dakota put her hands on her hips and tried to look threatening. "Please give it back."

"Why?"

"Because it's mine."

Maddy crossed her arms. "Describe your gift, and I might return it."

Dakota's cheeks flamed. "How can I do that when I

never got to open it? All I know is it's from Uncle Godfry, so I'm sure it's a beaut. If you don't give it, my mum is going to call yours. I've got witnesses."

"Believe me, your uncle's present was a snore. Matter of fact, I wrapped it right back up again. Stay here, I'll go get it."

In the next minute, she'd returned with the gift, its tissue refolded and twine retied. Dakota tore it open. "Oh." She lifted the object. "It's a . . . thingamabob."

"A clarinet," Maddy clarified. Which belongs to my big sister, she didn't add. But since Lexie was into guitar, Maddy figured nobody wanted to hear her play *two* instruments horribly. One was plenty.

Palming it off on Dakota was a genius idea.

"I don't play clarinet." Dakota looked confused. "Was there a card?"

Maddy felt itchy. Even for her, this was a lot of mischief for one day. "Yeah, but I guess I threw it away."

Dakota brightened. "Let me come in and poke around your rubbish for it?"

"Sorry, I only invite my friends inside my house."

Dakota pursed her lips. "What if I said I was your friend?"

Hope swelled through Maddy. She was surprised by it. Why did she care if Dakota wanted to be friends? Then again, what good was an imaginary friend like Susanality? "You can't just *say* you're my friend. You have to *be* my friend."

"But we're far from friends, Maddy," said Dakota. "You're a horror."

"You could give me a trial friendship," Maddy said. "Like for one day. Tomorrow, how about?"

Dakota's wispy brows knit together. "S'pose I could do *anything* for a day. But if we make that deal, it means absolutely, positively no vile tricks out of you."

Maddy considered this. All school year, she'd been the odd girl out when it came time to pick partners for science or lunch line. She always sat alone on the bus. She'd never been to a sleepover. Not that she cared. "It's lonely at the top," she always reminded herself—though she wasn't quite sure what she was on top of. And all this summer, while Lexie giggled with Pete and Hudson planned adventures with Duane, Maddy had been left to herself. School aloneness was one thing, but family aloneness was . . . lonely.

No pranks in exchange for one day of flesh-and-blood human friendship was as easy a swap as a cursed necklace for a new cape. "We'd be friends all tomorrow?"

"Quite right."

"I go where you go?"

"Gorgeous." Dakota always used festive words like that. Maddy figured it was an Australian thing.

"I do what you do?"

"Stunning." Dakota did look stunned. "You don't play golf, though, do you? Because that's what I'm doing tomorrow. We could always pick another—"

17

"I *looove* golf," said Maddy, who'd never played. "The card's up in my room. Top floor." She held open the door.

Dakota paused, then decided. She rushed inside and up to Maddy's attic.

"Ooooh . . ." Dakota's dark eyes were wide as a lemur's. "Damp. Bit like a cave."

"That's the idea," said Maddy, crossing her fingers that Dakota wouldn't run away. Lexie had warned Maddy that any mortal who dared to venture into this room would be too spooked to return. But Dakota seemed fine. Maddy scooped the card from her wastepaper basket.

Dakota read it greedily. "Must be more to this clarinet than I reckoned." She tucked the card in her pocket. "Thanks, Madison." She sounded so grateful that Maddy experienced a twinge of guilt. Followed by a twitchier twinge as she watched Dakota lift the clarinet and blow into the mouthpiece—probably still spitty from Lexie's last lesson.

The resulting honk of noise was awful but way better than Lexie's clarinet version of "Last Goodbye." Then Dakota lowered the clarinet and paused, her head bird-tilted. "I don't hear a thing," she whispered. "Do you?"

Supersonic-eared Maddy could at that moment hear a thousand sounds:

- A team of kids in one of Central Park's softball fields, arguing about who was safe on base
- Her parents around the block, returning home from

    band practice and discussing where they might have put the missing salad spinner
- Her brother in the kitchen, pouring himself a glass of cran-grape juice

"Sorry, nothing," Maddy said.

Dakota's plump shoulders slumped. "No matter. Uncle Godfry's cracked," she said. "He lives in remotest Yap, Micronesia, and he scuba-dives all day. Not sure why he sent me a clarinet. I hope this one isn't stolen."

"Yeah, me too. Okay, see you tomorrow," said Maddy.

"Thrilling." Dakota looked about as thrilled as a glass of milk.

Then she raced off, Lexie's clarinet snug under her arm.

From her doorway, Maddy watched her unexpected almost-friend-for-one-day stop at the next traffic light and, in the wait for the green, lift the clarinet and blow.

Though everyone who heard this awful noise was now glaring at her, Dakota's upturned face was so hopeful that Maddy almost, *almost* wanted to do the right friend thing, to run down the street with Uncle Godfry's *real* present and trade it back.

4

K IS FOR . . .

In the Old World, Lexie, Maddy, and Hudson had each slept in his or her own coffin down in their medieval cottage's cobwebby cellar. During those days, they'd relied on their animal instincts. Like many nocturnal creatures, their "sleep" was so light that the ping of a wind chime could rouse them, alert, prepared to flee the pureblood predators that slayed gentle fruit hybrids for sport.

In the New World, though, Maddy needed real sleep. The kind that made her drool and snore and didn't end until her battery was recharged. After all, she was on her way to fullblood mortality. As long as she kept up good human behavior, the Argos decreed that she'd lose every single one of her vestigial vampire traits by high school.

Sad as it would be to say farewell to her fangs and night vision, Maddy enjoyed certain aspects of mortality. She was getting older. And taller. In the Old World, after the Bite, she'd aged only one human year per century, a process so slow it was like staying the same age forever. But in the New World, Maddy aged one year per year. She even had a growth chart taped to her door, and she marked her progress every morning.

But tonight, Maddy's eyes were wide open, staring at the ceiling as thoughts stormed through her head. How early should she arrive at Dakota's apartment? Would Dakota's mother still be upset about the stolen gift, now that it had been (sort of) returned? Maddy kicked her covers.

It took her a while to realize that something else was keeping her awake. Her ears tuned in one part of the house, then another, until she got to Hudson's bedroom, from which crickety sounds were emanating.

Chhrrrrup. Clickity snick click . . . Distress clicks. What was wrong?

Annoyed, Maddy jumped out of bed and sped down the stairs. Hudson's room used to be a portrait gallery and still looked like one. Hudson had liked the oil paintings of grim, long-dead humans, so he'd kept them up. He never used his bunk bed, either, because he slept like a bat, dangling upside down from his double-jointed knees in the closet.

Maddy approached the closet door, where Hudson's DO NOT DISTURB sign hung from the knob. "But *you're* disturbing *me*," she hissed, stamping her feet.

"Sorry," her brother whispered from inside. "I've got news. I better call a family alert."

Family alert! That didn't happen every night. Maddy opened the cedar-scented closet and flipped her body upside down in the identical position to her bat-morphed brother. Within minutes, Lexie and their parents had also followed Hudson's sonic call.

"Will this clothing rod hold all our weight?" asked their father, eyeballing it nervously. "I'm not the scrappy young nightwalker I used to be."

"Try yoga, darling." Their mother yawned as she re-arranged herself to hang upside down by her sweatpanted knees. "This better be important, Huddy. I don't like being echolocated for no good reason."

"Then I'll get to the point." Hudson ruffled his neck fur. "The Ninth Knaveheart Leader has entered the New World. And he—or she—is very close."

The others gasped. The word *Knaveheart*, referring to the most powerful and despicable of all vampire species, hadn't been uttered in so many years that Maddy's ear-drums singed to hear it.

"Are you sure?" asked Lexie.

Maddy asked, "How do you know?"

"Orville says they've found rat husks," said Hudson. "The Argos is on alert." Orville was an aged hybrid who, like Hudson, could transform into a bat. He was also part of the Argos, a secret New World organization that watched over all Old World creatures who had renounced vampirism and sought New World sanctuary.

Maddy cowered. For a Knaveheart, a full-grown rat is the same as a refreshing glass of water for a human. A healthy Knaveheart meal plan depended on eight rats a day.

"Why's he here?" whispered Lexie.

"Only one reason," Hudson answered. "There's a

22

search on for the heir, the Tenth Knaveheart Leader, to take over the Old World Knave Kingdom."

"Ooh, the Tenth," said Lexie. "Ten is my lucky number."

"There's nothing lucky about this news," chided their father.

"I don't get it. There's a jillion vampires in the Old World," said Maddy. "A Knave's got tons more heirs to choose from over there."

"True, but in *The Gospel of Terrible Species and Unknowable Creatures*, the text indicates that the Ninth Knave will cross into New World in search of a successor. We can't say we weren't warned." Hudson flexed a claw. "Orville advises us to stay on the lookout."

"So not only is the Ninth Knave here, but the Tenth heir, too? That's two too many Knaves for my comfort." Their mother shuddered.

"It's funny, I was just thinking about writing my back-to-school book report about the Seventh Knaveheart, Vlad the Impaler," mentioned Hudson. "Since our summer assignment is to write about a brave leader."

"Hud, hon, I'm sure your teacher meant for you to write about a mortal leader," advised their father. "Someone more like that New World explorer, Daniel Boone, who chopped down forests. Knave Vlad preferred to chop off heads. He might give your class nightmares."

"I could write a comparative essay of *both* leaders," mused Hudson.

"Okay, this family alert is adjourned," said Lexie. "My knees are locking up."

When Maddy returned to her bedroom, she took out her hybrid-language, Old World copy of *The Gospyll of Trydrbllel Species & Unknwyble Chryttres.*

Flipping to *K*, she read:

KNAEVEHEARTS
A Briefe and Trewe History.

Pitie the soule who needes to reade uppe on the Knaeve! For the Knaeveheart Dynestie (1108–present) is the cruellest unbroken reigne of all the vampyre sovereignties, as welle as its most secrytive. The fewe times Knaeves have beene recognyzed, it was due to their strength, extryme nearsightedness, and propynsity to feaste on Rat bloode whilst lyttering the huskes for anyone to steppe upon.

After the appointemente of the Knaeve Heir, the male or femalle slayes his familey to prove that olde loyalties have beene severed. As a newe rule of terror begyns for the changed Knaeve, so shall the olde Knaeve leader be exiled to a moste remote seasyde location for a finalle death crumble.

In accordance with a ten-verse Storey-Poemme scripted in Cyrillic onto the foundation walles of the Château Duchem, in the Blacke Forest of Uze, Olde Worlde, we are destyned for Ten pureblood Knaevehearts, each ruling for one thousand yeares. Every Knaevish reign is more evyl than the laste, until by the end of the Tenth, the Worlde's light is fulley darkened.

Such grimm horrors cannot be escaped unlesse the Curse is splyntered bye an Equitably Trydrbllel Chryttre.

A moste restpectfulle translation of the entyre Storey-Poemme, "The Knaeveheart's Curse," was penned by Boris Afanasyev.

Snore. Yawn. Maddy skipped through Boris's translation of the first nine poems. She didn't like poetry. But when she got to the "Storey of the Tenth Knaeve," she stopped to read it as carefully as she could, picking over the Old World spelling.

Storey of the Tenth Knaeve (X)

Past Ninth Knaeve's rule of boundlesse wrath
The Chryttre takes a dif'rent path
O'er salty sea to Newe World green
Treeless, where Nine glides unseen.

A family sircle makes a pact
Defends the Knaeve from front to back.

The Knaeve Heir X
Is first made sick

With poison strings and practised picque
Glass-eyed witnesses daren't blink
In slumber, X's blood blacks to Knaeve ink.

A dimwit sircle makes a pact
Defends the Knaeve from front to back.

As night then falls to feast and dance
Diverted by a game of chance
A call is made upon phantom arms
To breake this curse's deadly charms

And spiral Knaeve
To dusty grave.

A violent sircle makes a pact
Defends the Knaeve from lies and fact
Glass-eyed ring should freeze this spell
Restore X from an outer shell.

And *that*, Maddy thought, as she slapped shut the book, was why she didn't read Old World. Too confusing. Luckily, there wasn't much "Newe World green" in New York City. As long as Maddy kept out of the major parks, she'd be safe from whatever awful fate was encrypted in that poem.

She stuck the book back in her shelf. Then she ran to her bed and buried her head under her pillow, pulling up the covers around her neck.

Knavehearts, yeesh. That brought back some traumatizing memories. Knaves were the most vengeful of all the vampire families. In the Old World, they'd kept an iron claw over land and castles, and they'd fight any hybrid claiming even minimal vampire power. In the end, it was better to be mortal in the New World, her family had decided, than fight pureblood Knaves for all eternity in the Old.

Now one was here, on the search for an heir. Maddy hoped the Knave would just hurry up, find that stupid Tenth, and hightail it back to the Old World, chop chop.

Until then, they were all in danger. Hybrids, rats, humans—everyone.

5

TUNNEL OF TERROR

All night, Maddy's nightmares fed her fears, which was why she overslept.

The next morning started badly, when she discovered the shorts and shirt she'd thought were clean-folded in her dresser hadn't changed position from when she'd dropped them in her hamper. Ew, and they still smelled like the Candlewick Café kitchen, where she'd helped Big Bill peel onions for his famous French onion soup with soy cheese.

In the scramble to get to the lobby of Dakota's Midtown apartment, Maddy also forgot to brush her teeth and hair.

"Why, Madison, you're looking bright-eyed and bushy-tailed!" Nora announced merrily. "We're happy you'll be spending the day with us!" Dakota, wedged behind her mother, agreed with a tiny nod. "Ready for some golf?"

Though Maddy meant to answer, "You bet!" when she opened her mouth, all that came out was a loud burp that smelled like the Granny Smith apple she'd gnawed on the way over.

Club Lullaby, where they'd be playing, was outside

Manhattan, in Queens. Dakota's mom was driving them, and they launched the drive with a lively game of I Packed My Grandmother's Trunk. It wasn't until they'd got all the way to *P* (Maddy had just packed Grandmother a putrid, puréed prune) and had turned into the Midtown Tunnel that Maddy realized she was breaking a golden rule: vampires should never cross underneath running water. Uh-oh. When Maddy got really, really scared—as she was right now this minute—she started to dry up.

"Water! Water!" Maddy gasped.

"Sorry, Maddy. You'll have to hydrate later," said Nora. "But Club Lullaby makes a lovely limeade."

"Aaaaaggghhh," Maddy wheezed. Her throat was already dusty. Her lips were cracked.

"What's wrong?" Dakota twisted around in the front seat. "Swallow your gum?"

"Release me from this most foul tunnel." Maddy twitched as Old World words confused her thoughts. She whipped out her asthma inhaler, which did no good, because this was a completely different issue.

Calm down, she told herself.

But she could feel her eyes starting to sink back into her skull. Oh, no—fear was sucking out her internal liquid supply. She was starting to petrify. The Argos had warned her about this. Hudson said that once he almost dried up at the dentist, when Dr. Wen found a cavity on his baby fang. He'd been so scared he'd run outside with the clip-on bib still hooked around his neck.

It had taken a lot of coaxing to get him back. Hudson didn't like the dentist. Too many centuries of bad memories, when dentists used wrenches, leeches, and lancets.

But there was no way to run out of a tunnel. Maddy was trapped. And if she got too dehydrated, just one thing would save her. The only available beverage in this car. Blood. Maddy began to unbuckle her seat belt.

"Madison, rules! Sit back and keep that seat belt fastened," warned Nora, but now Maddy's ears pricked as she heard Nora's heart pumping with nerves. A whirring sound, tantalizing as a cherry Slurpee machine.

"Hang in there, Maddy," encouraged Dakota, "and I won't tell kids at school you're scared of tunnels."

Maddy's eyes rolled wild. All she could focus on was Dakota's plump neck, her pulsing, juicy vein. "Hhhhhh-hhhh . . ." Maddy's hiss startled them all. The tip of her tongue scraped her fangs. She pressed her lips together.

"Breathe into your inhaler, sweetie," advised Nora. "There's a girl." But in the rearview, her wild eye caught Maddy's. Yet I'm powerless to stop, Maddy thought. She tried to fight the urge. Fortunately, at the same second that she lunged forward to snack on delicious Dakota, a light appeared at the end of the tunnel.

Relief. All fear evaporated. Maddy's claws instantly relaxed back into dimpled girl hands and Dakota's neck again looked like a grimy kid neck, no longer tempting as a caramel apple.

"Ahh." Maddy rolled down the window to drink in the fresh air. Close one.

30

Nora and Dakota still looked scared. And when had all these leaves blown into the car? Maddy looked around curiously. Why hadn't any landed on Maddy or anywhere in the backseat? Dakota and her mother seemed guilty as they shook the greenery from their heads, shoulders, and laps.

"Dearie me, that was a dreadful asthma attack, Madison," said Nora, plucking a leaf from her ear as they crossed the parking lot. "Let's find someone to give you a once-over. Just to be safe, all right?"

"Uh-huh." In the distance, Maddy saw a peak-roofed wooden house set on a smooth sheet of lawn. New World green, she thought. Where had she heard that phrase again? Then she remembered and gulped. Uh-oh. How could the Knaveheart's Curse have slipped her mind so quickly? New World green was all around. Her eyes moved to check out the tennis courts, shaded by silver pines. Woods looked safer.

If a Knave was around, the woods made a good escape route.

"'Club Lullaby, a Haven for the Young and Old.'" Maddy read the sign nailed to the clubhouse. A few of the Old were snoozing on the porch. "What kind of club is this?"

"It's a sports-and-hobbies club. They've got loads of rules, so just remember to say, 'may I,'" explained Dakota. "Sure you're up for a golf lesson, Maddy? P'raps you want to rest with the oldies."

"I'll be okay," said Maddy. She'd just keep off the widest, green-iest greens and hope for the best.

31

Nora led the girls past the clubhouse and to an adjacent bungalow marked CLINIC, where one of the staff coaches checked Maddy's pulse and reflexes.

"I'd make a lousy doctor. I can't even find her heart," the coach said, shamefaced. Maddy wasn't surprised—after the tunnel scare, the shy blip of her hybrid heartbeat would be too faint to locate.

She was relieved the coach didn't take her temperature, which, at fifty degrees Fahrenheit, might have given him an even bigger shock—and was why hybrids tended to stick to their own, Argos-approved doctors as they made the transition to mortality.

"I just need some fruit juice," Maddy promised. "Then watch out, Tiger Woods!"

"That's the spirit," said the coach, pouring Maddy a cup of limeade.

"Make it two," said Nora. With a weary wave for the girls, she retreated to the clubhouse porch with the other limeade loungers.

On a small putting green, the lesson was under way. A dozen or so kids, including Dakota, wheeled sporty bags stocked with golf irons.

"Ooh. Maybe I'll take this," said Maddy as she fished inside a pretty plaid golf bag and selected the shortest iron.

"Maddy, careful. It's not 'maybe I'll,' it's 'may I,'" explained Dakota. "As I said, you must watch your manners here."

"Hey! That's *my* golf bag." Lisi Elcris, in a minidress paired with fancy tasseled golf shoes, bounded across the green, her kid brother, Adam, rolling behind.

"Sissy Smellkris. What a frightful surprise." Maddy bared a hint of fang.

"I'm rubber, you're glue, what bounces off me will stick to you," said Lisi, stabbing her finger against Maddy's chest. Of all the New World insults Maddy had heard these past few years, Lisi easily claimed the lamest.

"As a matter of fact, Maddy and I are friends today," Dakota piped up.

"Poor you." Lisi stuck out her tongue as Maddy picked up her golf iron.

"Hey, that's mine!" Lisi squawked, reaching for the iron and jumping right into Maddy's first-ever practice swing.

"Oh—ouch." Maddy felt bad. She hadn't meant to connect her iron so smoothly with Lisi's kneecap.

"*Yowch!*" Lisi was hopping up and down. "You hit me on purpose, and I'm totally reporting you!"

"It was an accident," corrected Maddy. "And I said I was sorry, didn't I?"

"Technically, Mads, all you said was 'oh—ouch,'" murmured Dakota.

"You should sit this lesson out," bossed Lisi. But she'd stopped hopping, Maddy noticed, so her knee couldn't have hurt that much. "Besides, your clothes smell oniony. You're giving off fumes, and that's not fair to the rest of us."

33

Adam snickered. "Giving off fumes," he repeated.

"It's Club Lullaby that gives off fumes," said Maddy. "Loser fumes. You should rename it Club Stinks."

Adam laughed at that, too. "Club Stinks." But Maddy was mortified. Lisi could be such a bully. And she was ruining the Day of Friendship.

"I don't feel like playing golf," Maddy decided. It was too sunny out here, anyway.

"What will you do?" Dakota's dark eyes darted around, as if trying to anticipate what mischief Maddy might find.

"Eh, I'll figure out something. Come find me when it's time for lunch. Later, warts."

Whistling, Maddy kept her nose in the air as she strolled off the course. Probably best to get off these dangerously wide green fields, anyway . . . though her cheeks went beet red when she overheard Lisi talking in a loud voice about how she was going to tell management to banish Maddy from Club Lullaby for good.

She'll pay for wrecking the start of my Day of Friendship, Maddy decided. I'll strategize an excellent revenge plan. But first, she thought as she bounded up the clubhouse steps, more limeade.

6

A BOX OF DISGUSTING

One handful of uncooked oatmeal and molasses. Best cure for flatulence." Mr. Elcris wheezed on his words. He even sounded full of hot air, thought Maddy.

She was crouched under the Lullaby clubhouse porch, indulging in her most favorite sport, eavesdropping.

"Wild yams help my embarrassing gassy episodes," quavered Mrs. Elcris's high-strung voice.

"If you don't want gas, dear, you gotta skip the kidney beans," Mr. Elcris scolded. "I'd rather find a cure for hair loss."

"Oh, Stan!" Mrs. Elcris sniffed.

Gag. Maddy grimaced. Those Elcrises sure liked to have sickening conversations when they thought nobody was around. Eeeyyyuck.

She rolled out from under, taking with her the plastic litter she'd found to throw it away properly. Since Hudson was an environmental crusader, the Livingstones knew it was crucial to clean up the New World.

Though Maddy had been listening in for a long time, the kids *still* weren't finished with their golf lesson. Even under the porch, Maddy's skin was cracking from the heat. She needed moisturizer. She'd already had one scary episode today.

In the clubhouse locker room, Maddy dropped her porch litter in a recycling bin, where she found a shoe box marked with the Elcris Shoe Emporium logo for Lady-swing Premium Golf Cleats.

"Excellent!" In spite of where the box came from, any box had the potential to be treasure. Maddy fished it out and looked inside. No cleats, but a whole lot of paper tissue. She tucked the box under her arm. Good find.

Now to get her hands on some moisturizer. With her sharpest-bladed pinkie nail, Maddy picked all the locks down the row until she found a locker stocked with a full bottle of aloe lotion. She held it directly over her head and squeezed. Her skin, dry as a roadside iguana from scalp to toe, made a greedy, sucking sound as it absorbed.

Ah, relief.

Replenished, Maddy picked up a nearly empty mouthwash bottle. She let her hyperextended tongue roll all the way down to the bottom, soaking in the spearminty essence.

Ah, refreshing.

The wide-toothed comb of this locker was thick with hair, which gave Maddy her next idea, to create a Box of Disgusting. In the Old World, a Box of Disgusting was a dangerous tool, a hand-packed bomb of dust, dirt, hair, scum, lint, fingernails, earwax, tartar, belly button and toe jam, cigarette butts, and anything else that looked like it might be decaying or crawling with germs. A dash of Disgusting to the eye could inflict temporary blindness; a pinch in the ear could cause vertigo. And pity the stomachs of those who got Disgusting dissolved in their dinners.

Maddy remembered how she and her Old World friends, Elewynn and Hautement, had been legendary talents at creating Disgusting. Now, Maddy realized sadly, if she wanted to concoct something remarkably Disgusting, she was all on her own. As usual.

"But it might be just the right weapon if that Knave's on the loose," Maddy thought out loud. She shook the shoe box. "Fate even sent me this vessel."

After re-picking the lockers and stripping all combs and brushes of every flake of dandruff and strand of hair, Maddy roamed the entire locker room, unclogging the matted shower drains, plucking used tissues and Q-Tips, and, from behind a toilet, one spiderweb in which was a caught a shriveled caterpillar shell.

All into the box.

Next, windowsills. Experience had taught Maddy that the best icky stuff nestled in deep crevices. Sure enough. In went two dead scarab fighter beetles and a squished pod of chewed gum.

Maddy was so intrigued with her project that at first she didn't pay any mind to the voices drifting through the open window.

"It's not fair, D. We've been friends all year. I even let you wear my wooden watermelon bracelet for two weeks, and it's my most favorite thing I own."

"We're still friends, promise. Plus Maddy's not as bad as you think. She gave me back my birthday present, and here's a teensy secret about her—she's deathly scared of tunnels."

Lisi and Dakota! Maddy's skin itched worse than when she'd been struck down with scarlet fever, many centuries ago, during a deadly epidemic. No matter how many years Maddy had inhabited this earth, she always got sensitive when she overheard people talking about her.

"Madison Livingstone, scared of tunnels?" Lisi snickered. "I'll remember that one. But why'd ya have to bring her here?"

"We're not real friends, exactly. We're just for-the-day friends."

"I don't get it."

Dakota sighed. "Like, we're *being* friends. As an exchange of favors."

"Huh." Lisi snorted. "So you're fake friends. Whatever. I'm not jealous. Anyway, my super-fantastic cousin Zelda who's visiting from Denmark is my *best* friend *plus* we're family. She plays guitar better than anybody, and she makes us all homemade gazpacho every morning."

Ha ha ha. That Zelda already found a way cooler friend than you, thought Maddy, scoffing. And she happens to be my big sister, Lexie! She wished could shout that down to them.

"What's gazpacho?" asked Dakota.

"A delicious drink," Lisi assured. "And if you come over, I'll give you some."

The conversation turned to delicious drinks. Listening in, Maddy seethed. How humiliating, to be exposed as a fake friend! She kicked off her sneakers to hoist herself onto the windowsill. Her extra-long feet and double-jointed knees steadied her hind crouch-grip. "You girls are about to get totally Disgusting-ed," she muttered.

It wasn't until she was staring down at the unsuspecting tops of the two girls' heads that Maddy remembered her pact with Dakota.

No tricks, no pranks.

"Fie!" Maddy spat. Of course, she could break the pact, but the sticky issue was that vampires feel very loyal to verbal agreements. In Old World days, paper was expensive, and writing was a rare skill. Most people's word was their bond.

But Dakooty's word was worth nothing. She just broke her own promise by blabbermouthing that Maddy was scared of tunnels.

The Box of Disgusting tipped in Maddy's hand. How funny would it be if one beetle fell on each girl! She cackled to herself.

Suddenly, there it was. A vampirish knowledge, slipping through her skin, pricking up her ears and fangs. She was not alone in this locker room. Somebody—or something—was watching her. Somebody—or something—had heard her cackle.

Maddy looked up as the shadow passed over.

What was that? She froze. Slowly, her head circled, *click click click*, all the way around, in a complete rotation, as her eyes darted to every corner of the locker room. The lines of the poem slivered through her consciousness . . . *to Newe World green / Treeless, where Nine glides unseen.*

Whatever it was, it was gliding unseen, all right. Maddy's heart knocked in her chest. From below, her ears picked up the faint sounds of Dakota and Lisi standing up and walking away.

Swoosh! The creature zoomed in like a hawk, but a hundred times faster and a thousand times stronger as it grazed past, knocking Maddy off balance.

"Hey!" She swayed light as a leaf in the windowsill.

Swoosh! From the other side, the thing whipped past again, smacking so hard against Maddy that when she caught herself, *pop!*—like a cork from a bottle, her clavicle separated from her acromiun in a type I acromioclavicula joint dislocation (most vampires know the medical names of their bones) injury.

"That hurt!" Way worse than a clonk to the kneecap. Such brute strength was almost completely inhuman. Maddy shivered, her green-blue blood gone icy. The Ninth Knave. It had to be!

With one option, Maddy took it.

Swoosh! As the creature whipped past to clip her again, Maddy was ready. Flinging her Box of Disgusting over her shoulder and straight at the Knave, she bounced into a back handspring and vaulted herself out the window.

7

IN THE GRAVEYARD

Whoosh! through the air and *smack!* Maddy hit the ground hard. Her bones creaked. Her collarbone cracked. No time to check damages. She ran, not stopping until Club Lullaby was miles behind her.

Ancient vampire smarts led her way. Her bare feet slapped the forest paths and twisty dirt roads. And then she arrived in a place that more than made up for her terrible day, as Maddy stared across the paradise also known as . . .

"The Queens Calvary Cemetery," she said. "Wow." Her hands clenched the locked iron gates as she peered in, awed.

Magic. She'd heard about this place, one of the oldest and biggest cemeteries in New York State. But she'd never viewed it in all its moldering magnificence. Marble crypts and mossy, crooked tombstones as far as she could see.

"Here we go." She swung herself over the gate, dropping like a cat to the grass.

Maddy's last visit to a grave site was when she and Lexie had made a pilgrimage to the tombstone marker of doomed rocker Jim Morrison, who was laid to rest at

Père-Lachaise, in France. Almost all vampires loved Jim Morrison, and the Livingstones were no exception.

Most vampires adored cemeteries, too. Maddy imagined undead souls surrounding her like vapor. She strolled the rows of graves, reading names and dates, remembering her favorite vintage years and imagining these people as they might have been.

MOSES MINGUE (1742–1801)
EDWINA D. CARR (1913–1975)
JUSTAF LIPPMAN (1696–1714)

When she got to the tombstone of Giulio Rissetto (1689–1701), she leaned against it in order to crunch her shoulder bone back into its socket.

Then she sat down cross-legged on the tombstone plaque of Graham B. Murdoch (1823–1900) to consider what to do next. She had no shoes and no money. Between herself and home was a deadly current of water. And she'd made her blisters worse. Blue-green blood was crusted all over her heels and toes.

Losing blood was not only bad for her hybrid health, it might mean that the Knave could pick up her scent and track her.

"Yoo-hoo, Hudson!" Maddy called to her brother through echolocation. All of the Livingstones had retained this useful bat trait. Maddy didn't know where her brother was, and so she bounced her SOS into his general districts—home, Duane Rigby's apartment, and the Henry Hudson Parkway, where Hudson liked to fly free.

She called and called. Her echo didn't catch and dissolved to nothing.

Not good. By now, the Underhills would have contacted the authorities. After all, Maddy was missing, and in the New World, missing children got reported immediately—not like in the old days, when townspeople believed that if you weren't home by Sunday supper, you'd either moved to a new village or been eaten by wolves. In either scenario, there was no need to start a search party.

Not in the New World. People here thought a missing kid meant trouble.

"Mom!" she screeched. "Dad! Lex!" Mostly she kept trying Hudson. Ole Crud had the best hearing and would ask the fewest questions about what happened to her sneakers and why she'd been dumb enough to cross underneath water and nearly petrify herself.

"Help!" she called.

And now, at long last, a snag and a bounce—but not one she'd expected. "Madison! Climb up a tree, and I'll come get you on flyby."

Maddy jumped to her feet and looked around. The return caller was unfamiliar.

"Who are you?" she bounced.

Long silence.

"Hey, I'm not doing anything until you identify yourself," Maddy called. "I'm not supposed to bounce to strangers."

Longer silence. Then, "I'm no stranger. I am Orville of the Argos, on my way."

"Orville?"

"Your brother is too small to carry you."

Maddy bit her lip. Orville was Hudson's friend, and, being an Argos, he was uptight about New World hybrid rules. So Maddy tended to keep her distance from him. Hudson might be too small for the job—but would Orville really help a rule-breaking hybrid in peril?

Or what if this was a trick? If she climbed to the highest tree, she'd be exposed to that Ninth Knave like the dumbest bunny in hunting season.

Then again, if Orville *really* was Orville, he might just be her only hope.

"Get climbing," bounced the message. "I'm flying in fast!"

Maddy stood and brushed herself off. The sun was going down. Tree branches cast icicle shadows and tombstones threw shadowy blankets over the lawn. The miles she'd run had turned her leg muscles to sponge. She was hungry. She was too weak to save herself.

She'd have to risk it. No choice.

Maddy gripped the base of the highest tree, a red ash, and began climbing. Her palms still stung from her handspring. Heaving herself up, Maddy drooped double on the branch, like a wet towel on a line. Her neck swiveled for a sign of Orville.

The minutes ticked past. It felt like every tree had eyes.

A bat appeared in the distance, slipping through the dusk on leathery wings. Orville! No trick—she was saved!

And then, from the opposite side, another creature appeared in the distance. This creature, though farther off, was larger than Orville and sleek as an airborne panther.

The Ninth Knave.

Birds shrieked warnings and dived for cover.

"Up, Maddy, up!" Orville called.

Maddy's nails dug bark as she hoisted herself higher. She could hear the birds' hearts beating loud as a rainstorm. Her throat was going dry. Uh-oh. Fear was starting to petrify her again.

"Go away, Knave!" she called.

"UP!" Orville's signal was a sonic boom.

I'm trying! But Maddy was too exhausted to bounce more messages. The moon had appeared in the sky, and the silhouette of the approaching Knave was outlined sharp against it.

"Remember, the Knave can't see you!" bounced Orville. "Hide deeper in the branches, Madison. Keep still. Knaves are extremely nearsighted!"

Maddy reached and clung to a stout branch. The Knaveheart dipped and blindly circled the tree as Orville pushed forward, his claws attempting to snatch Maddy by the scruff of her neck. He missed.

Nooo . . . Maddy tried to swallow her scream, but a peep of despair escaped.

Instantly the Knave honed in, dive-bombing the tree. A

steely talon scraped Maddy's cheek. Ouch! She bit back her yelp. Swooping on an angle, the Knave smashed blind against the trunk.

Maddy squirmed as the Knave's wings shook off left-over crumbles from Maddy's Box of Disgusting—right on top of Maddy's head.

"Just drop!" commanded Orville as he circled back in. "I'll catch you!"

Maddy had to chance it.

She let herself fall, hands over knees over hands, branches slicing her arms and legs, sagging with relief to feel Orville's claws hook her by the shorts—even if this careful catch allowed a quick but rather embarrassing view of her underpants. At least it was dark.

And she was safe at last.

She wrapped her arms tight around the neck of the old Argos as they sped away, New York City bound, while the Knaveheart's caw echoed faintly through the cemetery. Alone and blindly searching . . .

8

MADEMOISELLE LIVINGSTONE, I PRESUME?

Nobody wanted to tend to Maddy in her mildewed attic, so the family decided to put her in Lexie's room.

"Argh, nooo . . . I'll recover way easier in my own bed," Maddy protested sleepily as her parents tucked her between Lexie's rose-scented, pressed cotton sheets.

The next morning, even before she'd opened her eyes, Maddy sensed the stamp of her sister's care. Starting with the itchy, high-necked nightgown that Lexie must have tugged onto her when she'd been too weak to fight it.

"Good morning, sister dear," sang Lexie as she slid a breakfast tray over Maddy's lap. A bowl of Big Bill's broccoli broth, a beet-ginger shake, and a fruit salad—a classic Lexie menu—were lovingly arranged. "Dad and Mom are working late today. They have double dog-walk duty," Lexie explained, "so I'm taking care of you till they get home."

Maddy's eyes cracked open. Her hand rose to touch her head. "Why's this weed stuck in my hair?"

"It's not a weed! It's a white gardenia, the favorite flower of doomed singer Billie Holiday. You looked so frail asleep that I tucked one behind your ear." Lexie pulled a face. "But now that you're awake, you don't look as romantic."

"Har har." Maddy yanked out the flower, then picked up the bowl and sipped. Broth was usually a tasteless excuse for food, but this morning, ah. She drained the bowl, then slouched back in the pillows and rubbed her head. "Yeesh. I was having such strange dreams about the Old World."

"That's because I was reading to you from *Narrative of an Expedition to the Zambesi and Its Tributaries*, by David Livingstone, the famous explorer who identified our vampire-fruit-bat nomenclature *Pteropus Livingstonii* and gave us our last name. Remember him?"

"Duh. Doctor Livingstone was the most important contact in our then-eternal lives. He helped us figure out what we are." Maddy scratched her lacy neck. "Why are you reading it?"

"Lexie was checking that your concussion didn't erase your memory after the Knave attack." Orville was sitting in Lexie's rocking chair, so motionless that Maddy hadn't noticed him.

Today Orville was in human form, where he was known by all as Mr. Schnur, a cranky old janitor at Hudson and Maddy's school. He was even wearing his janitor's green coveralls.

Maddy sat bolt upright in bed. Bits of the night rushed back to her. Wait—she hadn't been dreaming—she really *had* been attacked by the Ninth Knaveheart.

She looked at Orville. "Thanks for rescuing me," she said.

"You're not one hundred percent rescued." Hudson's voice was muffled. "Sis, you gotta be careful. Now that the Knave knows you, you're in more danger than ever." Lexie's window shade rattled as Hudson unrolled himself to land on the sill.

"Oh, whatever." Maddy waved off the warning. "Predators have chased us for centuries. I can usually take care of myself."

"Listen to your brother," warned Orville. "It's no joke, Maddy. I speak as a member of the Argos—and as a friend."

In agreement, Hudson clicked his displeasure and flew around the room, finally alighting on the bedpost.

"For someone who lucked out in the looks department, Hud, I don't know why you spend all your time as a bat," mentioned Lexie.

"Because Crud's a show-off." Maddy yawned.

"You're just jealous because I can bat-morph and you can't." Hudson preened.

"Well, you're jealous because I met the Ninth Knave," Maddy shot back.

"Um, I think you mean you almost got crushed and pulverized by the Ninth Knave."

"Maddy, you're obviously feeling strong enough to talk," interrupted Orville, leaning forward, "and I've got questions. Where did the Knave find you?"

"At Club Lullaby, in Queens," said Maddy.

"As I suspected. Don't go back there. We think it's the Knave's headquarters."

"Why there?" asked Lexie.

"A golf course is the perfect habitat for a near-blind bat, because there aren't any trees to crash into during flight," Orville explained. "For limited portions of time, Knaves are able to take on a human identity, and so our Knave could go to and from Lullaby undetected. Since rats love Dumpsters, there's also plenty of Knave food. Finally, a Dumpster makes a nice, private cave during a Knave's extensive sleeping hours."

Mmm . . . to Maddy, those Dumpster rats sounded a little bit delicious. In the Old World, she used to snack on tiny woodland creatures, and she still wasn't quite used to her family's strict vegan New World diet. In fact, when nobody was looking, she'd been known to slurp down the odd mosquito or fat tick.

Now she picked a chunk of papaya from her fruit salad, pretending that she was sinking her teeth into a baby field mouse. "Okay . . . but what's next? Is someone planning to slay the Knave?"

"No, no. Nobody's slaying anything. In fact, the Argos have been trying to negotiate a land treaty," said Orville. "If the Ninth Knave stays on one side of the water and we stay on the other side, we hope to maintain peace."

"For how long?" asked Hudson.

"As long as it takes for the Ninth Knave to find the Tenth."

"Hope that's soon." Lexie's lip curled. "I hate thinking of a Knave on the prowl."

"Yeah," Maddy agreed. "That Knave was kinda violent." She could feel her fingernails sharpen as she remembered.

"You won't be missed at Lullaby, Mads," said Hudson. "Your friend's mom was panicked. She called the police in all five boroughs. But everyone figured you ran away to sulk after you got kicked off the golf course."

"Everyone is wrong. I didn't run away to sulk. I was chased off by a hybrid-hating Knave. Hey, if I slayed that thing, I'd end their evil dynasty, right?"

"Madison! There's not a chance you could slay it. Stay out of its path, and let destiny run its course." Orville stood. "As always, this has been a top-secret conversation, for our sonic ears only."

Then Hudson sailed out the window, while Orville left through the door.

Maddy was too worked up to rest up. "I could so slay that Knave! I was caught off guard this time. Next time, I'd be ready."

Lexie, not listening, was strumming a guitar.

"Doesn't sound half bad," Maddy conceded, though it didn't sound half good, either.

"Thanks!" Lexie beamed. "It belongs to my guitar teacher, Zelda. She's letting me use it to practice. She's performing at the Candlewick Café at the end of the week, if you want to come."

"Uh-huh." Blech, an acoustic guitar concert? No way.

Maddy knew if she wanted to think up her Knave-slay strategy, she'd have to leave this room of tuneless, strummy music. She snapped back the covers and jumped out of bed.

"Where are you going?" Lexie glanced up, alarmed.

"Up to my room," said Maddy as she hopped out of bed. "Sorry, Lex. If I want to get back to my old self, I need to stop smelling the flowers and start smelling the mold."

She also wanted to see if there was any online information about Knavehearts. On her way upstairs, she detoured into the family room and ran a search on the computer.

Nothing. In the e-world, Knavehearts had covered their tracks so carefully, it was as if they had never existed.

A letter was waiting in the Livingstones' in-box. It was from underhillfamily@nycmail.org. Uh-oh. Maddy double-clicked and read:

G'day, Livingstones, this message is for Maddy:

Hi, Maddy,

Your mom told my mom you got in a scrape after running off. Are you okay? Mum was quite worried about the whole thing, esp. b/c she had to call the police and it was such a to-do. Is this the end of our Day of Friendship?

Yours,

Dakota

P.S. It was fun playing I Packed My Grandmother's Trunk with you. You came up with some goodies. Call or w/b.

Maddy flushed. Dakota had told Lisi they were fake friends. So why was she pretending to care if Maddy was feeling better?

No way was she going to call or write back. Instead, she hit delete. Fast.

9

SECOND THOUGHTS . . .
AND THIRDS . . .

Maddy!" her mother sonic-hollered. "Phone!"

Whoa! Stop the presses—who'd be phoning her? Dakota, maybe?

Maddy took advantage of the fact that her whole family was in the kitchen sharing a melon cup breakfast to slide down the banister from her attic all the way to the first floor. She hit bottom on her bottom in under ten seconds, nice!

"Hello?"

"Madison Livingstone!" boomed a voice. "Please come over for a brief visit. Your opera cape is ready. You won't be disappointed, so I suggest you bring your payment." Click. The caller had hung up before Maddy could get a word in.

But she knew who it was.

Maddy smiled. It had been a few days since her Lullaby fiasco, and she was ready for something wonderful to happen to her.

She ran back upstairs and fished in her hamper for some not-quite-dirty but still pleasingly smelly clothes and rounded up her walking cane, hat, sunglasses, her outgrown sneakers since she'd lost her other pair at Lullaby, and, finally, her von Krik necklace before taking to the street.

"Bye, everyone! I'm having breakfast at Susanality's," she yelled as she ran out the door. Thank goodness for imaginary friends. Although, Maddy decided, a real one would have been plenty okay, too. Guess not this summer.

Another hot day. In three blocks she was out of breath, but using the cane was fun. It clopped so loud that people stepped out of its way.

She used the cane to rap on the door of the tailor's shop.

A window screeched open as Carlyle looked down from above. "Mademoiselle Livingstone, I presume?"

"Here I am! *May I* have my cape?" Maddy upped her politeness by using a British accent. British people always sounded so polite.

Carlyle disappeared, and the door buzzed. Maddy bounded inside and up the stairs, panting with excitement.

"Normally I don't like to be too hospitable, because it gives the wrong impression of me," said Carlyle, "but you look rather dehydrated. Would you like a glass of water?"

"Sure."

She drank three glasses before she saw it.

"Ooh!" The finished cape, hanging from a mannequin dummy, was capital *S* Splendid.

"Lucky you're so short and a cape pattern is so simple," said Carlyle as he swirled the cloak off the dummy. "It took two yards of cloth and four hours of effort. But your sneakers look shabby for this cape. I suggest a trip to the Elcris Shoe Emporium."

"No, thanks," said Maddy. Yick, those Elcrises were everywhere.

Carlyle flung the cape over Maddy's shoulders.

As the fabric settled in a purple velvet column from Maddy's neck to feet, a long-lost sensation rippled through her. Yes, this was how she was supposed to feel. When the Livingstones had fled to the New World, they'd left too much of their familiar culture behind. Maddy loved her modern, New World comforts, but the cape whisked her back down the dim halls of Old World memories, reminding her of what she'd once been.

Powerful and predatory.

"Perfect," she said, hopping off the pedestal and fishing out her von Krik necklace for payment.

"Ahh!" Carlyle reached out and grasped it. "Exquisite!"

Maddy frowned. Perhaps it was the way the beads winked at her, as if they knew a secret, but something didn't feel right about relinquishing so rare a treasure.

Was it foolish to give up the only prize from the ashes of pureblood vampire Nicola von Krik?

She had taken the necklace because it was pretty and because it was vampire loot.

But what if it meant something more?

What if it could help her slay Knave Nine?

Carlyle seemed to sense Maddy's hesitation. His hand

swept the necklace into the sewing table's drawer, which he shut with a bang.

"Fun, fun, but now all's done." His fingers cinched Maddy's arm as he escorted her from his shop. "You're a funny little elf, but don't come back unless I invite you," he said, slamming the door.

Standing outside the tailor's shop, Maddy's heart raced with doubts.

"Here you go." A man, striding past, had stopped and dropped something into the glass of water that Maddy was still holding since Carlyle had rushed her out so quick.

"What the . . . ?" She held up the glass. A quarter rested on its bottom.

Then she got it. She'd been standing on the curb so silently, in her hat, walking cane, cape, and sunglasses, that the man had thought she was a blind person. He had mistaken her drinking glass for a change cup.

Intriguing. Maddy smiled as she fished out and pocketed her quarter.

10

BLIND GIRL'S BLUFF

A few days later, Maddy slid into the booth at the Candlewick Café, where Lexie was sharing a Garden of Diva smoothie plus bee pollen boost with her best friend, Pete.

From the starry brightness in Lexie's eye and the hang of Pete's head, Maddy suspected it was a kiss-and-make-up smoothie. Over this summer, Lexie and Pete had been in a lot more fights and make-ups than usual.

Sometimes Maddy thought their quarrels had to do with the fact that recently Pete had become a hottie. And hotness, as everyone knows, tends to bring out a lot of emotions.

"Sorry I'm late."

"You haven't missed anything. Zelda's just about to go on." Lexie pointed to the back of the restaurant, where a high stool and stand-up microphone had been placed.

"I'm surprised you're here at all, Madness. I didn't think you were into acoustic." Pete yawned and stretched. Now that she knew Pete was a werewolf, it made sense to Maddy why—when the moon was on the wane—he got tired so easy.

"Wake up, Pete. It's only lunchtime." Maddy snapped

her fingers in front of his face. He was only here because Lex had dragged him. Truthfully, Maddy wasn't at the Candlewick to listen to guitar music, either. She had bigger fish to fry.

All week, Maddy had been making tons of money from her great new scheme—pretending to be a blind beggar. Maybe she'd even earned enough to buy back the von Krik necklace from Carlyle.

Maddy knew the Candlewick was risky territory. For one thing, it was too close to home, and Maddy also had a hunch her parents wouldn't approve of her scheme. But now that she was here, in the presence of so many kind-hearted vegans, Maddy knew she'd be able to rake in some good moola.

She decided to work the room a little bit before the show. She stood, hobbling and tapping.

"Oops, I'm sorry!" Maddy exclaimed as she bumped into a man carrying a bowl of tofu turkey stew, the house specialty.

"No, *I'm* sorry," said the man. "Maybe it was *I* who jostled *you*. Here."

"Thanks." Cool, a dollar. Maddy tapped herself back to her seat. She waited for the next person to pass by before she jumped up and stumbled into her.

"Careful, honey," clucked the woman. "Poor thing. Your parents should get you a guide dog."

"That's what I'm saving up for." Maddy sighed. The woman looked sad and gave Maddy all the loose change in her coin purse. Yes!

Maddy rammed into a few more people, collecting their donations, until her sister signaled her over.

"Enough, already, Mads." Lexie reached up and snatched off Maddy's sunglasses. "That is a totally inappropriate summer job."

"Besides, it's an insult to real blind people, who would prefer not to be thought of as charity cases," said Pete. "And you can't just smash against strangers all afternoon and scoop up their pity money—"

He stopped.

Guitar in hand, an extremely tall and willowy green-eyed girl with curled-at-the-ends auburn hair had slid up onto the high stool that marked the performance space. She tested the mike and waved to a table up front. Maddy craned her neck. The Elcris family—bleh! They were way too everywhere.

"That's Zelda!" Lexie clasped her hands. "Don't we look alike?"

"Eh." Maddy could see it. All the parts of Lexie that didn't look like Maddy—such as Lexie's noodly limbs and plushier mouth—were mirrored in Zelda.

But Lexie's excitement irritated Maddy. Zelda wasn't Lexie's twin or even her sister. Maddy was. And in a summer when it had been next to impossible to make a friend, Maddy had been relieved that sisters didn't get a choice. They *had* to be friends. Even if one of the sisters pretended to be blind or gave away the other sister's clarinet. Sisters were forever linked. That was a rule. Or at least, Maddy had always counted on it being a rule.

"Ooh, I hope she sings 'The Rose'—the most tragic ballad in pop history." Lexie sighed.

Zelda pulled a black guitar pick from behind her ear and strummed a few chords. "Just want to give a shout-out," she said in a husky, accented whisper. "Thanks, everybody, for coming to support the arts."

She strummed her guitar and played a few songs. She had a near-perfect voice, Maddy decided. And aside from having musical talent, she *was* a lot like Lexie. Was it the earnest way she sang those doomed songs? Was it how her green eyes seemed to flash both at and through the audience?

When she was finished, everyone burst into loud applause—though the Elcrises were loudest of all.

"Thanks." Zelda smiled with the confidence of someone who was used to praise. "At my next concert, I'll be sharing the stage with my newest star student, Lexie Livingstone, who is also my dear friend."

"Oh my gosh." Lexie started to hiccup from excitement. Pete thwopped her on the back.

"So come over to Dolly World," said Zelda.

More clapping.

"Dolly World?" Maddy scrunched her nose. "Isn't that a department store?"

"Shh!" Pete put a finger to his lips. "An artist has to start somewhere."

After her last song, "The Rose," which Zelda dedicated to Lexie, the lanky teen enjoyed a final round of applause before she tucked her guitar pick back behind her ear with a flourish and loped up to their table.

"Here," said Zelda. She handed her guitar and pick to Lexie. "You can borrow it this week for practice."

Maddy tried to roll her eyes at Pete, but he was concentrating on being supportive, and so he just looked away.

After Zelda had gone, Lexie turned to Maddy. "Outrageous, isn't it? Zelda's exactly like me!"

"Not really. She's Danish and you're Plain-ish."

Lexie frowned. "You're so negative, Maddy."

Maddy fumed. She leaned back and dropped her Blind Girl's Bluff glasses over her eyes so her sister couldn't see the hurt in them. Of course she was feeling negative. And sour, and jealous. Why didn't Lexie get it? It was as if this Zelda had put a kind of spell on her sister. Maddy wished she could put a friendship spell on someone.

As it was, her Day of Friendship with Dakota had been a disaster.

And Susanality wasn't even a real person.

Was Lexie rejecting Maddy, too?

11

DOLLY WORLD

For the occasion of Lexie's concert, Maddy had decided to stay in her Blind Girl's Bluff costume—sunglasses, hat, cape, and cane—though she had mostly stopped looking to profit from her fake blindness. She'd made enough money. All she needed now was the courage to approach Carlyle and get that necklace back. She suspected it wouldn't be easy.

The three siblings plus Pete strolled down Fifth Avenue to where Dolly World took up almost an entire city block. Inside, it smelled like chocolate and peppermint and tinkled with music that chimed from a lighted carousel in the middle of the concourse. Dozens of moms, dads, grandparents, and babysitters were being led by squealing girls and boys, all shopping for dolls and doll merchandise.

Of which there was plenty.

Much too much.

"This place is more like a Dolly Universe!" Hudson whistled.

Maddy stared. From floor to ceiling, dolls stared back at her. Shelves and shelves of china, cloth, and plastic dolls. Baby dolls, girl dolls, grown-up lady dolls. All sizes, all skin tones. Dolls with auburn hair, blond hair, Afros, bun-headed, cornrowed, braided, bald. Dolls in every costume from bikinis to snowshoes. Hundreds of pairs of glass eyes, all on Maddy.

"'Dreamscape Dolly Theater.'" Maddy read the words off the directory. "It's on the second floor. Escalators up, thataway."

"How awesome that Lexie was asked to perform in a concert," mentioned Pete as they reached the theater and filed into folding chairs. "Even if it's only a concert for dolls."

"Think about it. Dolls don't have functioning ears," Maddy reminded. She'd heard Lex practicing earlier this morning, and she'd brought earplugs.

"Yeah, she can't be that good so soon, right?" Hudson wrinkled his nose. "In fact, it seems impossible that somebody who's been practicing for only two weeks—and who doesn't even own her own guitar—would be pro enough to play a concert."

"The important thing is to be supportive," said Pete.

Maddy nodded and stuck her earplugs in.

Moms and dads and girls and boys and dolls quickly filed in. It wasn't long before she saw the Elcris family slinking into the front row. Ugh. Maddy slouched down. Those Elcrises were inescapable. When Adam twisted around in his seat, Maddy bared her fangs. That set him straight again.

A few minutes later, lanky Zelda slouched to the front of the stage and said some things that earplugged Maddy couldn't hear. But she clapped along as Lexie came out and perched on the high stool and began to strum a few chords.

At first, Maddy didn't realize what was happening. Energy was rippling through the room. People were smiling. People were nodding and tapping their feet. People seemed to be . . . *enjoying* themselves.

Maddy popped out her plugs. Wait a minute. Lexie sounded gorgeous.

"Bravo!" Everyone clapped and whistled.

Instead of looking abashed, Lexie twirled Zelda's guitar pick behind her ear and allowed the adoration to wash over her as if she'd been performing in public her whole life.

Not a very Lex-ish reaction, thought Maddy. She was practically preening. Never had her sister seemed so foreign to her. Hudson looked taken aback, too. "It's like she thinks she's royalty," he murmured.

After the concert, Lexie hadn't lost her smug air. It wasn't even fun to congratulate her. "Yeah, I'm probably a better musician than Mom and Dad," she said with a little yawn. "Also, I think I feel like walking home by myself today. A true artiste needs some alone time."

"No problem, seeing there's not enough room on one sidewalk for you, us, and your swollen head." Hudson looked peeved.

They all watched Lexie cruise off.

"I wonder what's got into her?" Pete's voice cracked, as it sometimes still did when he became emotional but didn't want anyone to know.

"She's being pretty flouncy, though." Maddy's heart upticked. What was wrong with her sister?

At the corner, Maddy watched as Lexie nearly banged into a streetlight. When she turned, she stubbed her toe against a fire hydrant.

"Sorry, doggie," said Lexie as she patted the hydrant's top.

Was Lexie losing her sight?

And had her jeans always stopped so high above her ankles? Or was she growing taller? Also, as her hair caught the sun, it seemed to be lighter. In fact, it appeared almost reddish.

When she wasn't pretending to be blind, Maddy had the sharpest eyes in the family. She knew they weren't playing tricks on her. But Maddy decided to keep her fears quiet. After all, there could be lots of explanations. Lexie was having a growth spurt. Lexie was tinting her hair to Zelda's more-exciting auburn. It was pointless to jump to dramatic conclusions—such as the one that kept buzzing in Maddy's head, insisting that the mysterious Zelda had cast some kind of spell on her sister.

"Ole Hex is just going through a stage," Maddy reassured Pete as they trailed Lexie from a distance. "Girls can get like that. Even the most ancient and eternal ones."

12

THE SECRET OF THE ICE MIRRORS

Voila!" Her mother was smiling as she pried open the UPS box.

Maddy knew what was inside. The Dead Ringers' Graveyard Gates tour T-shirts. Their parents' three-city tour wasn't starting until October, but they'd been waiting for the T-shirts with great anticipation. It didn't seem like a tour until there was a T-shirt.

"Ooh, purple!" Maddy whooped.

"Worth the wait," agreed her mother. "Let's see. A size small for Hudson, a small for you, and a medium for Lexie." She scooped out the T-shirts.

"Lexie needs a large," said Maddy. "She got tall this week."

Frown marks appeared between her mother's eyes. "Jeez, Mads, you noticed that? I did, too. So I did some research, and humans don't grow *noticeably* in one week. I better take her to Dr. Harte and see what's up."

"Yeah, and if Lexie's going to be seven feet tall, you'll need to find the store that sells extra-long shoes, too."

Her mother nodded. "The Elcris Shoe Emporium specializes in footwear for the big and tall. We'll get you some new sneakers, too."

That name again! Maddy didn't say that she had boycotted the Elcris Shoe Emporium and anything else to do with horrible Lisi Elcris. "Mom, does Lexie seem less Lexie-ish to you?" she asked carefully.

"Yes." Her mother sighed. "It's been on my mind. According to my research, she's in this mortal stage called 'terrible teens.' And I don't think it helps that she always hangs around with that hormonal Pete Stubbe." She unpacked the rest of the T-shirts and flattened the box for recycling. "I'll call the doctor today. Probably you *all* need checkups. And speaking of checkups, I think you should check in with Dakota Underhill. Her mother was so worried about you, and she keeps calling. You still haven't apologized, have you?"

"Mmm," said Maddy.

"I mean it, Maddy."

"Mmm."

It took all morning for Maddy to make the call.

"Oh. Hi, Maddy . . ." Dakota sounded nervous.

"Since I only spent half my Day of Friendship with you, I wanted to come over and spend the other half. Okay?" Maddy could feel her face turn hot—a horribly human trait. Back in the vampire days, she never blushed. She tried to get the apology out, but it seemed to be stuck like a cherry pit in her throat.

"Um, okay." Dakota's voice was faint.

"Good. See ya later." Maddy hung up.

The worst thing about going to Dakota's apartment was that Maddy couldn't take her fabulous walking cane. But she could show off her cape. The velvet was heavy for the middle of July, but it matched the purple letters of her new T-shirt that spelled out DEAD RINGERS—THE GRAVEYARD GATES TOUR.

Down the hall of the twenty-fifth floor of the building where the Underhills lived came a delicate music. Music that got louder as Maddy came closer but ended the moment she rang the buzzer.

Dakota opened the door. In her hand was Lexie's clarinet. "Mum's at work," she said. "But come on in."

"Great." Whew. No mom meant no apologizing.

Dakota's apartment was the darkest and coldest that Maddy'd ever tipped a toe inside. "Brrr!" It was like being trapped inside Big Bill's deep freeze.

All the lights were off, the blinds were drawn, and the curtains were closed against any hint of illumination. Maddy's fangs and fingers tingled to their tips.

A dreadful thought soaked up all the other thoughts in her head. Were the Underhills purebloods? Had she walked into a trap?

Impossible. For one thing, mirrors hung everywhere. And mirrors, of course, are a vampire's enemy. Unless the Underhills were a vamp species that Maddy had never heard of.

Dakota was eyeballing her. "You want cocoa?"

"Ooookay." Fear slid like the point of a claw along Maddy's spine.

As she followed Dakota, she flipped up her cape collar. What was up with all these mirrors? Full-length, oval,

69

skinny, mottled. Mirrors in heavy gilt frames, mirrors propped against walls, mirrors hanging on thick portrait cord, mirrors leading all the way down the hallway. Just as strange, a carpet of leaves and twigs was scattered loose over the floor.

Dakota was whispering over her shoulder. Maddy spun around.

"Who are you talking to?"

"You." But Dakota looked flustered. "I w-was just asking if you prefer milk or water for your cocoa?"

"Water." Milk, gross. Fruit hybrids and dairy products did not mix.

The air was cold enough that Maddy saw her own breath in it. She trailed Dakota to the kitchen. Vaporous currents slid past like gauze. Mirrors were so thickly ice-frosted that Maddy couldn't have seen her reflection even if she'd had one. She tightened the cape around her shoulders. It didn't stop her teeth from chattering.

Dakota, busy at the stove top, was whispering again.

"Who are you talking to?"

"Me? Nobody."

"Huh." Maddy didn't believe it. She began to prowl, swooshing around the kitchen, kicking up leaves, checking under the chairs and table and behind the hutch. Every time she sneaked up on another space, she snarled, "Aha!"—only to find nothing.

But there was a presence here. Maddy's animal instincts sharpened. "Dakooty, who else is in this apartment with us?"

"Nooobody," Dakota insisted. "La la la." She began to sing at the stove top as she stirred the cocoa. She picked a leaf out of her ear.

Nervous singing. The sign of a lie. Leaves sprouting from ears. The sign of . . . what!? Maddy remembered the car trip to Lullaby and how Dakota and her mom had brushed all of those leaves off their laps.

Maddy waited until Dakota had handed her a mug of hot chocolate. "Drink up."

Quickly, Maddy made her eyeballs drain of color, dark to light brown to gray to clear. "Tellmewhoyouare."

Dakota's eyeballs were harder than rubber. *Boing*, Maddy's trick bounced off them, ricocheting her own hypnosis back on her to trap her in a trance that was instantly paralyzing and not much fun.

"Your eyes are transparent—that means you're part vampire!" Dakota gasped.

"Your eyes refract trances—that means you're part ghost!" Maddy gulped, ten seconds later, once she was released from the spell. Creepy! She wasn't used to being tricked. Or frightened. Especially by kids her own age.

She backed away from Dakota. "Okay, game's up. Who are you, for real?"

"I'm a hybrid," Dakota admitted, advancing. "Otherwise known as the Australian ghost dryad. Mom is part dryad, otherwise known as a tree nymph. My dad is a ghost. Oh, but don't run off just yet, Maddy. You haven't finished your cocoa."

"A ghost? Your mom married a ghost?" Maddy wasn't

71

sure she'd ever heard of that before. Was it the cold or her nerves that were making her teeth chatter?

"They eloped. Mom was a landscaper at the hotel that Dad was haunting," Dakota explained. "Ghost marriages are the special privilege of dryads, as you know."

Maddy had thought that was just a rumor. Being part ghost and part tree nymph seemed more exotic than her own mix of vampire–fruit bat.

"If your mom's a dryad and your dad's a ghost, then what are you?"

Dakota looked pleased with herself. "Mostly human DNA, with some ghosty traits, and I'm dryad-ishly good at climbing trees. Plus I shed leaves when I'm feeling emotional—I got that from my mom."

"Yeah, I noticed."

Dakota plucked a tiny leaf from her nose. "There're many of us in Queensland, so we had heaps of friends. But Mom and Dad wanted me to get to know more mortals. So we all moved to New York. Once Mom gets old and dies, she can join Dad in the afterlife. Then she'll be with him always."

"Okay, but . . . where is he now?"

"Haven't you guessed?" Dakota pointed. "Dad's in the portals."

"Mirrors, you mean?"

"Not precisely mirrors. They're passages to the Other Side. Dad comes out on special occasions, but like all ghosts, he needs to stay where he belongs. We keep it cold so he can see us and write us messages through the frost. Look—there's one now."

Maddy's eyes darted toward the portal, and she nearly jumped out of her sneakers at what she saw.

The words on the surface of the mirror were jagged, as if traced by a single, frozen finger.

PLAY A TUNE.

"That's a message from your dad?" Maddy asked.

"Yep." Dakota smiled. "Dad's always around. He's a stay-at-home ghost."

"He's asking you to play clarinet?" Maddy wanted to stop trembling, but it was difficult. She wasn't sure she could stay one more minute in this haunted apartment.

"No, Dad wants to play a tune for you. If I face him while holding the clarinet to my mouth, the notes travel into my breath. Simple, really."

In all her centuries as a nightwalker, Maddy had witnessed just about everything, but rarely a trick as odd as the one Dakota proposed.

"Interesting," she said, with some doubt.

"Dad might be a little shy. We're not used to company." Dakota sat in an armchair and motioned for Maddy to take the ottoman next to her. As Maddy sat, she pulled her cape around and tucked up her feet. On the off chance Dakota's ghost dad was a biter. Most ghosts thought biting was funny, though it clearly wasn't.

The frost thinned. In the glass appeared the image of a young man.

"Ooh." Maddy gaped. He was perched in an armchair that was a replica of Dakota's, and he held a clarinet. The only extraordinary thing about him—besides his ghostliness—was that he had one foot stuck in a paint bucket.

"Why is your dad's foot in a bucket?" Maddy whispered behind her hand.

"That's where it was when he died," Dakota whispered back. "He was painting the hotel roof when he tripped over that stupid bucket. He fell forty-six floors."

"Sorry," said Maddy.

Dakota's dad allowed a sad smile, then raised the clarinet to his lips. Then, as Dakota mimicked his movements, he began to play his ghost clarinet, and Maddy realized that this was the same exquisite tune she'd heard earlier, when she was waiting for Dakota to open the door. The piping notes melted away Maddy's doubt.

After he finished, Maddy jumped up and whistled through her teeth. "Woo-hoot! Your dad rocks!"

By then, the glass had frosted over. Dakota's dad bowed and vanished.

But Dakota was beaming. "I haven't had such a lovely afternoon in ages."

"Me either." And because it seemed like the right time to say it, Maddy admitted, "I'm kind of a hybrid, too. My whole family used to be vampires, but we weren't born that way. After the Bite, we had immortality and sustained ourselves on a part-blood, part-fruit diet. When we moved here to New York, we got the chance to exchange our immortality for a vegan lifestyle. We're losing our vampire traits slowly as we build up our mortal blood."

"Wow." Dakota smiled. "So we're both hybrid immigrants. That's cool."

In that moment, it seemed to Maddy more like a real-friends smile than a fake-friends smile, though she couldn't be sure.

"How about let's go to my house now?" suggested Maddy. "No offense, but your apartment is colder than a hangman's heart."

Dakota nodded. "Let me fetch my moleskin cloak. They're all the rage among Queensland dryads. I don't wear it in the New World because I'm trying . . ." She lapsed into silence. Maddy could guess what her half-a-day friend was too timid to say. Dakota wouldn't wear her moleskin because she was trying to fit in with humans. Maddy knew all about that.

They strolled down the sidewalk, elbow to elbow. Dakota's cloak was long and olive green, with a peony pink lining and pink tassels. It billowed like a sail alongside Maddy's wave of purple. A breeze snapped the capes higher, and as they crossed the street, Maddy could feel everyone's eye caught by the splashes of color.

Dakota and Maddy exchanged another smile. Old World–style capes rocked.

Even Hudson seemed impressed when Maddy caught sight of him staring through the living room window. Hmm. Odd for Hudson to be in boy form.

But her brother had opened the front door before Maddy had a chance to pull out her house key. Something was wrong.

"Most sage sister," said Hudson in the Old World language he often defaulted to when he got tense. "'Tis many a flummoxed moment I've awaited your arrival."

"What's up, Crud?" Maddy asked.

"A vexing and curious—"

"In plain New World, please."

"Uh, sorry," he stammered. "It's Lex."

"My big sister," Maddy explained.

"Something's wrong with her. Not even Pete can get her to stop. Come upstairs and see for yourself." Hudson looked Dakota up and down, his eyes widening in surprise. "You too, Susanality. I didn't realize you were one of us."

13

LEXIE AT LARGE

Lexie had grown—more. That was the first thing Maddy saw. Then she noticed that the walls of her sister's bedroom were tar black.

"Your parents let your sister paint her bedroom black?" Dakota blinked, dazzled, as she stepped inside. "Lucky!"

"When did the paint job happen?" asked Maddy.

"I did it myself, last night," said Lexie. Her arms were moving like windmills as she threw books, notebooks, and her beloved vintage clothing into a couple of open garbage bags.

"Should I text your parents?" whispered Pete. "They're at the recording studio. They probably have a right to know that their oldest child has gone berserk."

"Not yet," Maddy whispered back. "They're *really* busy. And she hasn't done anything destructive."

"Yet," muttered Pete.

They all watched in silence. But when Lexie dumped out her bowl of potpourri, Maddy had to speak up. "Hex, why are you chucking out your fave smells?"

Her sister stopped and squinted. Her eyes had nearly doubled in size. They shone with a darkly emerald hue.

Her hair had lightened further, to maple syrup brown with auburn tints.

"I'm not chucking them. I'm losing them," said Lexie in a husky voice. "Remember—'The art of losing isn't hard to master. So many things seem filled with the intent to be lost that their loss is no disaster.'"

"Uh, sure. Whatever you say, Lex." Maddy wasn't fooled by the charm of the quote. Her heart went into overdrive when she saw that her sister's teeth glistened a translucent pink.

Lexie's attention moved to her mosquito net curtains, which she began to yank down.

"Dearest sister, no! Those curtains took you a fortnight to sew and countless hours to drape just right," Hudson protested.

Dakota was less perturbed. "Wow. Is your sis the black sheep of this family or what?"

"Not even close." Maddy was indignant. "*I'm* the black sheep—Lex is the goody gumdrop!"

"Well, she's a licorice-flavored gumdrop today," said Dakota.

Hudson sidled over. "Examine the fingertips," he whispered.

Maddy jumped forward and grabbed Lexie's hand. Lexie swatted her. But not before Maddy had seen. Sliced into every single fingertip of Lexie's right hand were green-blue welts. "How'd that happen?"

"Leave me alone." Lexie snatched back her hand and

She tore down the stairs and motioned Dakota to join her in the hall outside her sister's room.

"You've been to Lisi's apartment, right, Dakota?" she asked quietly.

"Sure, lots of times."

"Cool." Maddy retied her cape tassels.

"What's going on, Mads?" asked Pete as he stepped into the hall, Hudson close behind. "I can tell you've cracked a clue."

Maddy put a finger to her lips. "I think Zelda's the Ninth Knave and she's transferring power to Lexie. It's all in the book. From *glass-eyed witnesses daren't blink* to *poison strings* and *picque*. Doll's eyes and guitar strings and picks, that is."

They stared at her. "A Knave? Like Vlad the Impaler? But . . ." Hudson shook his head. "No way. Lex is just a girl."

"So am I, but I'm the only one in the family with the ruby-and-gold Slayer's pin. I destroyed the von Kriks, re-member?" Maddy arched an eyebrow.

"Point taken. What do we do next?" asked Pete.

"Crud—you come with me. Pete, you watch Lex. Don't let her leave the house or let her fall asleep—or else her blood will start to go Knave-y."

"Where are we going?" Hudson asked.

Maddy slapped Dakota's back. "My *friend* is going to show us the way. We're off to pay a little visit to the family Elcris."

14

THE FAMILY ELCRIS

You're flat outta luck, kids," said the doorman. "The Elcrises are all playing golf at Club Lullaby."

"Is their cousin Zelda with them?" Hudson asked.

"Oh, yes. She likes it out in the country air. She says she found a good nap spot." The doorman shook his head. "You know teenagers. They love their sleep."

And so do millennial-old Knaves in dark, smelly, rat-infested Dumpsters, thought Maddy.

"Plan B," she decided as the threesome headed outside. "The King Kong route."

"You mean climb the building? But the Elcrises live on the ninth floor," squeaked Dakota.

"Hudson and I've spent centuries scaling heights," said Maddy. "We've still got our excellent vampire skills. And you said you could climb trees. Think of the building as the highest tree you ever climbed."

Dakota looked uncertain. "I'll try."

They decided to scale the back of the building that faced into the alley. That way, nobody would see them. Jumping and swinging from ledge up to ledge was a test of the most flexible hybrid grip and strength. Maddy went first to test and show the route.

"This feels very scary—and illegal," huffed Hudson from behind.

"For humans, sure." Maddy was too busy counting floors to pay him attention. Her vampire traits were out in full force. Sharpened teeth, double-jointed bones, and a steel grip in her fingers. Scaling buildings had been a primary Old World activity, when they'd looked for predator-safe places to roost. "This apartment isn't even close to the challenge of climbing Notre Dame, remember, Crud?" she encouraged.

"Mmph," came the reply from below.

Finally, the ninth floor. Maddy wrenched open the window and plop, plop, plop, they all dropped inside, to find themselves in a supply room.

"The Elcrises live at the end of the hall," informed Dakota as they stood and dusted themselves off. "I'll lead the way."

"Here's a question," said Hudson as they tiptoed down the corridor. "If Lexie's fate has been written into the *Gospyll*, then isn't it her destiny? Which means that no matter what we do, we can't change it?"

"Go ask a philosopher. I'm interfering with Lex's destiny no matter how it's been set up." Maddy was already kneeling to pick the Elcrises' lock.

"The Argos really don't like it when you break and enter," warned Hudson.

"Well, I really don't like having my sister's identity transfused," said Maddy.

The lock held fast. "Cagey Knave," said Maddy. "Zelda's

83

on to us. She hybrid-proofed the locks. Not even the family skeleton key could get us inside."

"Hey, I think I can help," said Dakota. "My dad's a ghost, remember? When I wear this cloak, I can pass through doors."

Passing through doors? No way. The perfect spy technique. "Seeing is believing," said Maddy.

Dakota closed her eyes, pursed her lips in concentration, and pressed all her fingers against her chin. Slowly, the pond green fabric of her cloak began to change, becoming slicker, thinner, permeating the pores of her skin until Dakota herself had taken on a green and filmy dimension. She stepped through the Elcrises' front door as if it was made of water and was gone.

A simple click and then the door swung open. Dakota gave a small bow as she stepped aside to let them pass.

"Nice!" Maddy and Hudson high-fived her as they trooped through.

The apartment was dark. In the kitchen, a blender had been left to soak in the sink. "Lisi told me her cousin makes fresh gazpacho every morning," said Dakota as Maddy let her tongue unroll to test the rim.

"Seems that the secret ingredient in this batch of gazpacho is . . . rat blood. Blech." Maddy made a face for the others' benefit, though she secretly liked the taste.

"Rat blood!? Ew! That's worse than any of your food-swap tricks." Dakota grimaced. "Lisi's room is at the end of the hall. She'd have to share with Zelda, because there's no spare bedroom. Follow me."

"Locked," Maddy pronounced, testing it.

Hudson lifted an eyebrow. "Okay, do your thing, Susanality."

Again Dakota slipped through the door like mist and opened it from the inside.

Lisi's bedroom was pinkly, girlishly pretty.

"Not a fun place for a Knave guest," Maddy mentioned. She herself cringed at all the frills and flounces. Zelda's few possessions—her guitar and some songbooks—were stacked neatly in the corner.

Maddy opened a songbook, *Doomed Tunes for the Faint of Heart*. Inside, she found a pamphlet for Edgewater Retirement Condominiums in Jacksonville, Florida.

"Proof," Maddy determined.

"Of what?" asked Dakota.

"That Zelda's not really a teenager, but a soon-to-be retired old Knave," explained Hudson. "She's finishing up the last days on the job, training the new blood. Meantime, she's looking for a quiet place to rest."

It didn't take long to find the rest of what Maddy sought. In the back of the closet was the box for Ladyswing Premium Golf Cleats—also known as the Box of Disgusting.

Maddy rubbed her hands together. Apparently Zelda wasn't so cagey if she'd chosen Maddy's very own Box of Disgusting to hide . . .

"The poison pick." As Maddy lifted the box cover, the guitar pick gleamed like a spade. "That's how Zelda is changing identities with Lexie. When Lexie presses this

85

pick between her fingertips, she's morphing her hybrid print into Zelda's Knave one. Then when she presses the poison strings, they cut into her skin and transfuse her blood."

Hudson stared button-eyed at the pick. "Nice work, Mad."

"Thanks. I'll steal this pick to be on the safe side, but I think it's already done most of its damage." With great care, Maddy used the edge of her cape to lift the pick from the box, and then she tucked it into the pocket that Carlyle had sewn into the lining.

"Psst! People! And they're heading this way!" whispered Hudson as Maddy's ears picked them up, too, from inside the elevator as it pinged to the ninth floor. She recognized those voices. The Elcris family. Mr. and Mrs. plus Lisi and Adam. The whole unsuspecting, Knaveheart-harboring gang.

"Up and out," commanded Maddy as she jumped and swung into the windowsill, then opened the window. "Good, a fire escape. Move quick!"

Hudson, already in bat form, flew through the window to alight on the ledge.

Maddy checked over her shoulder for Dakota. "Chop chop!"

"Nooo." Dakota's eyes were two pools of fear. "I said I was good at climbing *up* trees," she squeaked. "But I'm all thumbs at getting down."

"Eeeee! I hear keys jangling." Hudson fluttered. "They're coming in!"

Maddy snapped her fingers. "Ghost-glide through that wall into the hallway, and then you'll have to take the elevator."

"Oh, okay." *Thump. Slam.* Dakota hurled her body against the wall. "Except I can't."

"What do you mean, can't?"

"When I'm nervous, my ghost traits don't work as well." Dakota continued to slam herself. *Bump. Thwump.* A green sprig fell out of her ear. *Thunk.* "My scared-er, dryad side takes over." *Thud.*

"Twenty feet. Sixteen, fifteen feet. Fast approaching. We're outta time," said Hudson. "Sorry, Susanality. Gotta fly." He flapped away.

"Get ghosty, Dakooty!" Maddy commanded, panic prickling her arms.

"I can't. Go, go!" said Dakota, shooing Maddy off. "It's way worse for you to be caught. I'm not enemies with any Elcrises."

Maddy's thoughts pinwheeled. True. But she shouldn't leave her friend in peril.

"I'm serious. Go!" hissed Dakota.

Maddy went—but not out the window. It wasn't fair to abandon Dakota. She dove back into Lisi's closet just as the bedroom door flew open.

15

ALAS, ASLEEP

What are you doing in my room?" Lisi demanded, using just as crabby a voice as Maddy would have expected.

Maddy pressed her ear to the door. On the sly, she had to admit that she was excited for this fight. She always got furious when Crud and Hex stepped an uninvited foot into her room—and they were family. She couldn't imagine the temper tantrum that spoiled Lisi might throw.

"I'm super sorry," said Dakota. "The doorman let me in. He, er, thought you were at home."

"Well, we weren't. Jeez, look at all these leaves you've tracked in here. And why're you wearing that dog barf green cape?"

Dakota sounded apologetic. "My mom made me wear it. When it's this hot, she worries about the ozone."

A moment of silence. Then, "Well, if you want to know the truth, D., I'm relieved you came by," Lisi said softly.

Huh? Maddy's eavesdropping ear itched in surprise. She *was*?

"You *are*?" asked Dakota.

"Yeah, I thought you'd dropped me to be friends with

that tiny gargoyle, Maddy Livingstone. Here, I even picked up a ticket for you."

"For me? Thanks," said Dakota. "What's it for?"

"Club Lullaby's Summer Solstice. It's a fancy dance and raffle tomorrow night. I thought you could sit at my table with me and my family. Including my cousin, Zelda."

"Oh, lovely." But Maddy could hear a wriggle of doubt in Dakota's voice. "Where is this mysterious cousin of yours?"

"Zelda's not mysterious. She's great. She sleeps a lot, but when she's awake, she's superhumanly talented at playing guitar. We didn't even know we had any relatives from Denmark. You should try one of Zelda's gazpachos— they're a Danish delicacy. Speaking of, wanna eat lunch with us? Dad bought pizza and cannolis."

"Lovely," breathed Dakota. "What's a cannoli?"

"They're like éclairs, but better. Once Adam ate five cannolis and got sick on himself. It was grr-ohsss!"

"Grr-ohsss!" Giggling, the girls left the room together.

Maddy fumed as she opened the closet door, swiping a bunch of Club Lullaby dance tickets off Lisi's bureau before she leaped out the window and skimmed down the fire escape. Here she'd tried to help Dakota, only to be traded away for pizza and a couple of cannolis! Her cloak snapped out behind her as she strode home.

"Anyway, I've got more important things on my mind," she said. "Like saving my sister." She stared at the tickets in her hand. She'd only snitched them to be mischievous, but suddenly the lines of the Knave poem floated like a banner across her brain . . .

As Night then falls to feast and dance / Diverted by a game of chance / A call is made upon phantom arms / To breake this curse's deadly charms / And spiral Knaeve to dusty grave . . .

Hey! Lullaby was having a dance and raffle. And a raffle was a game of chance, just like in the poem.

But where were the phantom arms? The only phantom Maddy'd met this week was Dakota's dad, and he was stuck in his portal. Could he be called out to break the curse? Could he help spiral the Knave to a dusty grave? And *which* Knave? The last thing Maddy wanted to do was send her sister spiraling.

At the house, more terrible news. Pete and Hudson were sitting on Lexie's bed. "Alas, she's asleep," said Hudson.

"No!" Maddy slapped her hand to her forehead. "Then Lexie's blood is blackening to Knav-ish ink. The dire destiny is coming true!"

"I'm sorry, Mads—it happened so quick, it took me by surprise." The pupils of Pete's yellow werewolf eyes had enlarged, like two worried eclipses. "Right in the middle of trashing her pressed-fern bookmark collection, she collapsed. Now she won't wake up."

Maddy peered over. Wrapped from head to toe in mosquito net curtain, Lexie lay like a chrysalis, openmouthed and snoring.

"No, no, no! Wake up, Lex!" Maddy jumped up and

down. "Fire! Police! Hey, Lexie—you're late for karate class!"

"I already tried all that. It's no use," said Pete. "I've also put her hands in ice water, pinched her . . . I even let a silverfish crawl up her arm." Pete bit his lip. "I really thought that'd do the trick."

"She's *still* growing." Hudson pointed. "Behold. Her shirt cuff buttons are popped, and her toes have broken through the tips of her boots. See?" He pinched Lexie's exposed big toe. Then tickled it. Nothing.

"Oh, poor Lex. She looks so uncomfortable, too." Maddy patted her sister's limp hand. She felt helpless. Of all the rotten destinies.

"Let's pull off her boots and replace them with her fuzzy bunny slippers," suggested Pete. His voice cracked. "She loves those bunny slippers."

"Good idea." But as Maddy leaned down to retrieve them, she spied more than her sister's fuzzy bunny slippers under the bed. Also pink, but not cute, that rubbery tip of . . . uh-oh, was it really . . . ? Maddy pronged her fingers. By the end of its fleshy tail, she lifted up a dead rat the size of a soda can.

The guys drew back in disgust. "Nasty."

Maddy swung the rat like a pendulum, testing its weight. Light as a husk. "Guess this is what stained Lexie's teeth pink. She must've chugged it." Maddy sighed and dropped the rat in a trash bag. More proof—vigilant vegan Lexie wouldn't harm an ant, much less drink a rat.

"What happens if Lex turns Knave?" Pete asked. "Be honest. I can take it."

"She'll have to give you up," said Maddy as she pulled off Lexie's boots and replaced them with the slippers. "Knaves are land robbers and plague spreaders. Pretty much the opposite of anything you'd want to be around."

"But I want to be around Lex more than anybody else," Pete burst out. "What can we do to stop the transformation?"

"Good question." Maddy wished she had an answer. Pete looked like he was going to melt with anxiety. "Our best lead is tomorrow night at Club Lullaby. Zelda's performing. We've also got her guitar pick. Maybe we can use it as a lure to make her re-transform Lexie. Zelda can take any other heir. But not my sister."

"And if she doesn't cooperate?" asked Pete.

Maddy shrugged, though inside she quaked to say it. "Then it's war."

"War? What kind of cock-a-doodle plan is that, Mads? You can hardly cross the water to get to Lullaby without petrifying," Hudson reminded.

"We might only be hybrids, Crud, but we've still got some awesome vampire energy!" Maddy burst out. "Where's your Old World fighting spirit?"

"Maybe you should tell your parents about all this," suggested Pete. "They're part vampire, too."

But Maddy and Hudson knew better. If their parents found out, all they'd do was tell the Argos, who'd hand over Lexie as quickly as loose change. One hybrid vampire sacrificed for the good of many.

"It's not the Argos we need," said Maddy. "It's phantom arms, from the line of the poem."

Pete looked puzzled. "Do we know any phantoms?"

"One," Maddy admitted. "And I'm not exactly sure how to get hold of him." Nor did she much want to. To get in contact with Dakota's dad meant getting hold of Dakota, and Maddy was still mad about how her almost-friend had run out on her.

But now was not the time for grudges.

Maddy squared her shoulders, then marched upstairs and made herself sit down in front of the computer. Flexing her fingers, she quickly typed:

Dear Dakota,

I need your help. A lot.

Please come over tonight. Bring your ghost dad.

Thanks.

Maddy

P.S. I forgive you for trading me for cannolis.

16

DOUBLED DANGER

Nothing's waking her up tonight," pronounced their father that evening. He and their mom were standing outside Lexie's bedroom. "Thought my edamame-and-red-pepper salad with mustard vinaigrette'd do the trick. Guess my girl's got more growing to do."

"*Too* much growing," her mother said with a sigh. "Her appointment with Dr. Harte is this Thursday." She shut Lexie's door. "And not one day too soon."

Maddy and Hudson exchanged a worried glance. Even though they'd decided not to alert their parents, they hated to see them so distraught.

"Night, kids." Their mother kissed the tops of their heads. "We've got a long day of rehearsal tomorrow, so please check in regularly on your sis. And tell her to call us when she wakes up."

"Sure thing," they chorused.

After their parents retired for the night, they ran back into Lexie's room and opened her window. Dakota was waiting on the leaf-strewn ledge. A clarinet was sticking out of her backpack.

"Thanks for coming," Maddy said.

Dakota smiled like it was no big deal, but Maddy's heart swelled with appreciation. It took a lot of bravery for Dakota to come back to a house with a changeling Knave in its walls.

Now Dakota removed a square of ice-packed glass from her bookbag and propped it against a chair.

"Afore mine eyes—a reflecting mirror!" Hudson hissed. He covered his face with his arms.

"Chill out. It's a portal," explained Maddy. "Dakota's dad is a ghost. We need him to coax Lex out of her trance."

"Ooh . . ." Hudson watched as Dakota's dad's image took hold in the portal. As Dakota began to blow into the clarinet, her father played, too, and the room filled with music.

In her bed, Lexie stirred, then yawned.

Dakota paused in her playing. "Is she knotted to the bed?"

"Uh-huh. Crud and I did it. Lex has got to stay put. If she wakes up, she'll want to find Zelda. But she'll never escape these knots." Maddy was glad she'd learned some rope tricks during the three weeks she'd spent in the Elf Scout troop. Her "triple-Houdini" plus "drowning-the-cat" knots were the next best thing to steel cuffs.

Dakota resumed playing. One haunting tune melted into another.

Come on, phantom arms, Maddy begged silently. Break the curse. But then Dakota's father stopped and Dakota leaned forward, pressing her ear to the portal.

"Dad says that Lexie's too deep in her trance. If he wanted to help her, he'd need to come to the Other Side."

"Oh, tell him he's totally invited!" Maddy exclaimed.

But Dakota was shaking her head. "It's not that easy. He'd have to be summoned."

"What does he need—a magic word? A secret code? I bet I could find it in my Old World recipe book. Wait—where's he going?"

"He's fading," said Hudson. "Nooo . . . come back." But Dakota's father was gone.

With a sorry sigh, Dakota began to repack her book bag. "Dad needs to be called on from a higher authority than us to cross to the Other Side."

Maddy smarted. "How insulting."

Dakota looked unhappy. "I'm sorry we weren't more of a help."

"Me too," Maddy agreed.

Dakota looked unhappier. She shook a scattering of greens from her hair and slipped through the room, gone before Maddy could offer her a late-night lemon-mint fizzie.

"If you want Susanality to be your friend, you gotta get friendlier yourself," Hudson remarked as they headed for the kitchen, where Hudson prepared their fizzies.

Maddy scowled. She disliked taking friendship tips from her younger brother. She dragged the Old World recipe book from the top back of the refrigerator. "I think

I've got the Lullaby transportation answer," she decided. "You're getting doubled."

"Me?" Hudson wriggled. "Why?"

"Why not double your strength? The only reason Orville flew me across the water last week is because he's not a weenie."

"Orville is also double my height and weight," said Hudson. "No recipe in that book can double me. Hey, let's cross over to Lullaby by hot air balloon. It's a quaint old form of transportation, and we'd land right on the lawn—Mads, what are you doing?"

"Concocting the Doubler. Sorry, bro. Balloons are pricey. Besides, you've got the wings—you're going to have to suck it up, double up, and fly me over." Chef Maddy was already pulling out ingredients for the juicer. Kale, parsnips, turnip, baby bok choy, red cabbage, and one large, violet beet all went into the pile.

"I hate 'snips," Hudson commented sourly as he watched.

Maddy put a finger to her lips. "Shhh—I think I hear Lex."

"You do? I don't." But Hudson rushed off, leaving Maddy alone to stir in the rest of the ingredients. Additions she knew her brother would *not* enjoy—such as chewable vitamins, two tablespoons of wheat germ, and a teaspoon of cod liver oil.

She dumped in a cup of blueberries to hide the taste, then added a shot of Tabasco for kick.

"'Set to jell overnight,'" Maddy read. "Cool. Nothing to it."

"Lexie's fine—if you count being in a Knav-ish coma fine," Hudson reported as he reentered the kitchen.

"We'll get her back. Lexie's too fruity to go Knave. Zelda picked a terrible heir to the bloodline."

"Actually," said Hudson quietly, "I think Lexie might be a great choice." He cleared his throat. "Maddy, I think she's a shifter."

"Shifter?" Maddy looked up sharply. "What's that?"

"Orville told me about it. A shifter has the power to take on the persona of other vampires and hybrids," said Hudson. "Which is why, when Lexie is around Mom and Dad and us, she's the fruity sweetiest. That's how we want her to be."

Maddy thought. "But when she ran up against the von Kriks, she helped de-poison them. Her anti-pureblood instincts weren't on guard at all." Maddy was still bothered to think about how her sister had helped those rotten Kriks recover from her garlic cookies.

"Exactly. Under Zelda's influence, it's been easy to transform Lex into a talented musician, which is what she's always most wanted to be." Hudson looked grim. "Just between us, I'm scared to defend Lex. Especially since a transformed Knave always slays her family to show that she's cut the old ties."

"Oh, that's just an old Knave's tale." Maddy tried for nonchalance, though she feared what Hudson said was true. But she and Crud had to stay brave and stick to the plan. If they wanted to save Lex, they didn't have a choice.

• • •

They decided to sleep on their roof that night. The temperature was perfect. Pigeons, doves, and bats sniffed out the Livingstone kids as their own kin and came to roost near them. Maddy loved it. She missed her coffin, that hunk of Old World oak where she'd dreamed away the sunlit hours. She'd loved being up all night, stargazing with the other nocturnals.

Soon the roof crowded with creatures. Maddy allowed a pair of doves to curl up in the crook of her arm. She fell asleep listening to her brother chattering and sharing leftover apples with the squirrels.

By dawn, Hudson had morphed into bat form and was hanging upside down between a pair of fox bats. Their pointy faces were peaceful. The morning dew beaded on their still, folded wings.

Slipping soundlessly inside, Maddy checked on Lexie. When she tried to readjust the pillow, her sleeping sister let out a caw as a trickle of Knav-ish black bile ran down the corner of her mouth. Maddy's heart was heavy to see it.

"Lexington, I know you can hear me," murmured Maddy. "Please stay put! I'll fix this, I promise."

In the fridge, the Doubler had thickened like custard.

Great. A strength-giving pudding for Crud. Taking care of this family was hard work.

Back in her room, Maddy pulled out from under her mattress a twist-tied Baggie nearly full of loose change plus assorted dollar bills, the sum total of her Blind Girl's Bluff profits. Drawing on her cape, she then sped out the front door.

Ten minutes later, she was picking the lock to Carlyle Blake's tailor shop. A quick pick; no hybrid-proofing problem there.

It was too early for the tailor to be in. Maddy lost no time removing the von Krik necklace from its drawer.

"Ah." She smiled to feel the necklace in her hand again. She never should have bartered this beauty. As a vampire relic, if there was any chance at all that the necklace might help save her sister or destroy Zelda, then Maddy had to take it.

The beads winked dully in the sun. Perhaps it was all the time they'd spent in Carlyle's drawer, but their color seemed to have faded. After a few minutes in Maddy's palm, the hue had shifted to a more Maddy-friendly shade of purple. Interesting. These beads had Old World power, which was exactly what Maddy needed. She was glad they were in her possession again.

Sad as it was to give up her coins, the exchange seemed fair. Carlyle could use the money to buy himself more fabric. Maybe enough for a couple of capes or another one of those biscuit yellow hunting jackets pinned to his mannequin dummy. Carlyle certainly had an eccentric clientele. Hunting was such an Old World pastime. There were hardly even any horses here in New York City.

Aha! Maddy's next bright idea made her smile. Thoughts of horses put a spring in her step as she hurried home.

But when she burst into her sister's room, she came face-to-face with a mound of pink mosquito netting and some loosed ropes—and no Lexie. Her super-strengthened sister had escaped.

17

STEED FOR THE DEED

So I've got one missing almost-Knaveheart sister and one bloodthirsty, Knave-hunting sister?" Hudson buried his face in his wings. "Lex is in Zelda's clutches by now. O dark and inevitable Knave destiny! It's too big a disaster to consider."

"Then don't consider it as one big disaster. Think of it as a handful of small dilemmas. Four, to be exact. We've got to get to Lullaby, detect our Knave from her double, reverse the curse, and bring Lex back intact."

Hudson snorted. "You make it sound so easy."

"Meet me at the front door by sundown, and tell Mom and Dad you're going over to Duane Rigby's apartment for a sleepover."

"And what should we say to Pete if he comes looking for Lex?"

Maddy'd already thought that through. "The moon is full tonight. Pete usually lays low when he turns wolf. Being a werewolf is hard to explain to your friends and neighbors."

Hudson swallowed. "I'll try to track him down. Times like now, I'd like to have a werewolf watch my back."

"My yumsgusting Doubler should help out, too. Come downstairs and try it."

In the kitchen, Maddy spooned him a sample.

Hudson made a face. "Ugh. That tastes worse than I'd have thought."

"Luckily, you don't have to drink the rest. I found a better candidate. We'll need to pit stop at Central Park before we head to Lullaby."

Maddy used the day to crack her parents' dusty Old World books, looking up the information she thought she might need most. Hard work, especially since she didn't like to read—or memorize. But to be a slayer, she had to be a scholar. Tonight would test if she had the Knave-fighting skills she hoped coursed through her hybrid blood.

She quit the books as the sun lobbed low into late afternoon. It was time to dress for the dance. Up in the attic crawl space, Maddy dug in a trunk until she found a lightweight sundress plus a pair of long riding boots.

Over the dress went her trusty vampire cape.

Into its pockets, Maddy carefully tucked her asthma inhaler, the von Krik necklace, and Zelda's guitar pick. Lastly, she tucked her walking cane under her arm.

"Ready as I'll ever be," she decided.

Hudson was pacing downstairs. He himself had dressed dramatically in a brocade Russian sarafan, a tribute to one of Lexie's tragic fiction favorites, Dr. Zhivago.

"I'm hoping Lex will catch the reference and remember who she is," he said. "I've tried getting hold of Pete, but I think you're right—he's hiding from the moon. Is Susanality coming along?"

Maddy shook her head. "Too dangerous. She's part dryad, after all. A Knave would chew her up and spit her out like a toothpick."

Together they headed for the park, arriving at the southeast entrance just as the sun was disappearing. Horses and carriages were lined up, waiting for tourists to request a scenic city ride.

"Look for a white horse," said Maddy. "White horses possess the purest magic. Also, a horse is the most ancient transportation—after dragons and unicorns. Which means that if we ride a horse over the water—"

"—you'd have the least possible chance of petrifying. Good thinking, Mads." Hudson pointed. "How about that one?"

The horse didn't look magical. Knock-kneed, more chalk dust gray than white. Its driver was tipped back in his carriage seat, snoring.

"She'll do," Maddy conceded.

As they advanced on the horse, Maddy leaped into the seat alongside the driver. "Hello, sir! Could you tell me the name of your magnificent steed?"

"Huh? Her? Er, that's Princess." The driver sat up, his baffled eyes staring into Maddy's suddenly-gone-clear ones, the last words from his lips before he fell into a trance that gave Hudson enough time to unhook the heavy brass axles that kept the horse fixed to its carriage. Princess was free.

"Yeah!" Hudson pumped his biceps manfully. "Check out these guns! I should enter a competition!"

Meantime, Maddy had scrambled from the driver's seat.

"Here ya go, Princess," she crooned, holding up the bowl of Strength Doubler.

At first Princess jerked her head. But then Hudson, who'd swiftly changed into a bat to navigate the ride, hovered close enough to speak in her ear. Princess listened to the plan, then whinnied agreement. The drink was gone in two horsey slurps.

Maddy leaped onto the horse's back. It had been nearly a century since she'd last ridden a horse, but the skill hadn't left her. She spread her vampire cloak over them both and under her breath recited the Nightwalker's Dusk Spell.

"This should keep us in an invisible state for thirty minutes," she told Hudson. She looped and tightened the reins just as Princess's driver snapped out of his trance, shocked when he saw that he was sitting in a detached carriage, no horse in sight.

With Hudson circling near her ear, guiding her, Princess, now double her strength, picked up her pace. Galloping over the Brooklyn Bridge via its walkway, Maddy sensed the water rushing beneath her.

"Stay calm," she told herself. She thought brave thoughts. Like slaying Zelda. By the time they'd touched land, night had fallen. A moonlit sky and lisp of wind. And another, odder sound.

105

"No creepy noises, Crud," grumbled Maddy. "Tonight is serious."

"I swear, I'm not doing that," protested Hudson, propelling himself higher. "I hear it, though. Like a twanging and blowing and hum, all together."

As Princess slowed, so did the sound. Maddy shivered.

The lights of the main clubhouse twinkled ahead. Windows had been flung open. Music was playing. As soon as Maddy stopped Princess by the kitchen Dumpsters, Hudson dive-bombed behind a holly hedge to reemerge transformed back into the doomed Russian.

"Livingstone *voskres!*" battle-cried Hudson.

"Shhh!" Maddy warned. She opened the Dumpster and dove in. A pile of rat husks told the tale, as well as a small handbook, *100 Easy Danish Phrases*. "The spine's hardly split," Maddy noticed, flipping through it. "Huh. Of course the Elcrises would never have questioned Zelda's story. They're so clueless, they think rat-blood gazpacho is a Danish delicacy." She slipped the phrase book into her cape pocket.

"Looks like we found Zelda's Lullaby nap spot," said Hudson as he helped Maddy out. "But no Zelda. Keep your eyes open. She's got to be close."

They sidled into the clubhouse via its glass ballroom doors. The room was filled with festive, dressy Lullabyers, chatting and clinking drinks. Maddy saw a few people dancing, while others lounged at scattered tables. And there, at the far end of the room, was the sight Maddy'd been dreading. The Elcris family and their guests of honor, all at a single table, were enjoying dinner.

Maddy heard Hudson suck in his breath. Her own ancient heart ached. Sitting side by side, Zelda and Lexie looked long and slim as two string beans. Their hair, pinned back in diamond clips, curled at the ends like apricot seaweed. Their eyes were bright as green sea glass. Their spangled silver dresses clung to them like stardust and spiderwebs. Neither of them was exactly Lexie, but neither of them was exactly Zelda, either.

"They look absolutely identical," said Hudson. "Any idea which is which?"

"Nope." Maddy shook her head. "One of them will pass on her title and go crumble in a condo in Jacksonville, Florida, and the other will reign as an evil sovereign for the next thousand years. One of them I need to slay, and the other I want to transform back to my favorite sister in the whole, entire world." She sighed. "You'd think there'd be a hint of difference."

When Lexie and Zelda turned their twin set of emerald eyes on Maddy, her hybrid instinct told her to run and hide. Their power was fearsome and startling. It took every drop of courage in Maddy to stand her ground.

"It's all right," said Hudson. "Remember, they're Knaves. Too nearsighted to see us." But they ducked behind a ballroom column, anyway, taking teeny peeks.

Not teeny enough. "Uh-oh," said Maddy. "We've been spotted. Here comes trouble."

Lisi Elcris, her beady eyes laser-focused, was fast approaching. On her one side rolled Adam. On her other, and looking very tentative, was Dakota.

"Surprise, surprise." Lisi smirked. "I didn't expect to see you Livingstones at our Lullaby soiree. May I hang up your coats? Or, in this case, your cloaks? This way to the cloakroom."

She herded them so bossily that they had no choice but to troop after her.

"Hold on to your stuff," Maddy murmured, but Hudson had shaken off his Russian cloak and handed it to Lisi, who flounced off toward a small door under the staircase.

A warning tolled in Maddy's ear. She kept her own cape tightly tied.

"Wait! Come back," she called, but Lisi, who was a head taller than Maddy, had opened the cloakroom door. She pushed Hudson inside, and then, just as smoothly, she pushed Maddy.

"Whoa!" Maddy's fingers reached out to steady herself in the door frame.

"Lisi!" Dakota squeaked. "What do you think you're doing?"

"Get with it, D. This isn't some tacky ice-cream store birthday party, where just *anyone* can come. This is an exclusive club, and no stinky Livingstone is welcome in it!" Lisi's long arm shot out, shoving Maddy, who wobbled for balance.

"An exclusive club!" Adam crowed, with an extra pudgy

push on Dakota, who veered into Maddy, who couldn't stop herself from slipping.

"Eeeee!" Dakota squeaked as she tumbled past Maddy to fall down, down, down, bumping and rolling.

Too late, Maddy realized that this wasn't a closet. It was a set of stairs.

"There! Now you two can be friends forever!" Lisi giggled and snickered.

"Friends forever!" Adam's snicker mimicked his sister's as they both slammed the door so hard that Maddy completely lost her grip and began toppling backward . . .

18

WHAT A DIDGE CAN DO

Thumpity thumpity thunk. Youch. Maddy hadn't taken such a dive since she'd gone tray-surfing down the staircase of her own home last January, in the days when it had belonged to the von Kriks. She'd been in grave danger then. She was in graver danger now.

Her bones reverberated as she landed hard at the bottom of the steps, smack next to Dakota, who was balled up and whimpering. "Maddy, what are we going to do? We're trapped!"

"Trapped? Trapped?" Hudson, who had shifted into bat form, was in a stupor of confusion, bumping around the cellar. Not graceful at the best of times, he was especially inept when he freaked out. Which he was doing now.

"Oof!" He flapped, flustered, as he blundered into a sagging shelf of fig jam and raspberry jam preserves. "There's no way out of here. O doomed us."

"Stop being batty, Hud," said Maddy, swatting at him. "We've got to figure out where we landed and how to escape."

"It's the Club Lullaby storage cellar," said Dakota, looking around, "but it's as horrible as a dungeon. Oh, dear. If only I had my moleskin cloak, I could slip through and rescue us. Instead, we're going to rot in here like Bastille prisoners."

"Don't even joke about that." In the Old World, Maddy often had swooped through prison bars, where she had seen many of the doomed and dying shackled to stone walls.

Leaping up the steps, she tried to pick the lock. No such luck. It was hybrid-proofed.

On the other side of the door, Lisi laughed. "So close, and yet so far." She snickered. "I'm gonna hang this key right here on its hook for when I'm ready to unlock you. *After* the dance, that is. My cousin Zelda instructed me to chuck you down there. She even predicted you were planning to wreck the dance and her happy reunion with her long-lost twin sister. Later, suckas."

"Later, suckas!" added Adam.

"Oh, this is just great." Maddy stomped back down the stairs and began to pace. The family Elcris wasn't to blame. They were just playing out their role, blindly defending their Knave and her twin—the green-eyed changeling formerly known as Lexie Livingstone.

As she kicked the wall, Maddy used her boot as a lever to turn a flip. "Ugh." She looked at Dakota. "If you'd playacted like you were Lisi's friend, you could've sneaked back and unlocked us. Now we're stuck down here, with absolutely no game."

Sniffle, sniffle. "I'm sorry. I don't know how to playact friends."

"Yes, you do," Maddy snapped. "Remember our two half Days of Friendship?"

Sniffle, sniffle. "After we started to try to help your sister, it wasn't playacting to me anymore. We were real friends, mostly."

Maddy stopped pacing. Really? she thought. "Maybe it's a tiny percentage of a fraction my fault we're in this mess, too," she admitted. "If Lisi liked me better, she wouldn't have gotten so pushy."

"True," agreed Dakota.

Hudson, in boy form again and wearing oversized waiter's clothes, had popped up on the top of a boiler tank. "The worst part is that we were foiled by the dimwit family Elcris." He sighed. "Adam Elcris is in my class, and he's a toad. He wears a new pair of shoes every day of the week. Plus he bites. I should have known he'd harbor a Knave."

"No regrets. Let's think." Maddy had taken out her walking cane and was using it to test the walls for hollow spaces. The concrete reinforcement was thick. She stopped tapping and looked up at her brother. "Crud, why are you wearing that outfit?"

Hudson shrugged. "There's a big pile of waiter uniforms by the washer-dryer. I thought disguises might come in handy tonight." He pulled at the black pants. "Even though they're not my style . . . The pants are cut very narrow . . ."

"Our sister is about to embark on a millennial reign as the leader of the most deadly pureblood vampire clan and you're worried about narrow pants?"

112

Her brother looked sheepish. "I'm really not much of a warrior."

"No kidding." But Maddy and Dakota changed, too.

She folded up her cape. "I'll come back for you later," she promised it.

As she turned to execute another backflip, the cane slipped from Maddy's hand and rolled across the floor.

"Ooh! Aces!" Dakota squealed as she picked it up. "Why, it's Uncle Godfry's didgeridoo!" Her eyes slid to gaze suspiciously at Maddy. "Why do you have this?"

"You gave that cane to Maddy, remember, Susanality?" said Hudson.

"And you can borrow it anytime," said Maddy with as much nonchalance as she could muster. "No biggie."

Dakota clutched the cane to her chest. "Borrow what's already mine, you mean?"

"You can't take back what you gave," said Hudson. "That would be very babyish of you."

"But look, my uncle had it monogrammed for me!" squealed Dakota. "Gertrude Dakota Underhill!"

"Wrong. The letters on the cane stand for 'Grrr, Don't Use,'" said Hudson, but he looked at Maddy, who shrugged. It had been a good on-the-spot lie, but not a great one. "Gertrude Dakota Underhill?" Hudson repeated, making a face. "What a lame name."

"Yeah, I prefer what you've been calling me," Dakota said shyly.

"Say no more, Susanality," said Hudson. "I'm happy

to relieve you of your name shame, especially since you're Maddy's very first non-imaginary friend. But now answer this. Why would your uncle give you a cane?"

"Because it's not a cane," Dakota explained. "It's a didgeridoo. No ordinary one, either. Uncle Godfry is Dad's brother. He specializes in making special didgeridoos that can contact the afterworld. He told me he'd send me one if I ever got lonely in New York."

"Is he, um . . ." Maddy cleared her throat. It was almost too good to be true. "A higher authority?"

Dakota's eyes met hers. "I believe so."

Maddy felt awful. A ghost-summoning didgeridoo was a way better present than a chintzy, used clarinet. Unfair swap. Luckily Dakota seemed so happy to have it back that she wasn't holding a grudge. She lifted an end of the instrument to her mouth and blew.

From its opposite end came a familiar twanging, humming, droning noise.

Maddy's ears perked up. "That's the same noise that we heard outside on the way over here. It must have been the wind blowing through the whatchamacallit that made those haunting sounds."

"Not a whatchamacallit, a didgeridoo!" Hudson looked excited. "Also known as a drone pipe. It's an ancient Aboriginal wind instrument. Wow, I never saw one in real life before."

"There's more to this didge than music," said Dakota as she blew again.

Was it Maddy's imagination, or had the cellar become

exceptionally freezing cold? She began to tremble. Something was happening.

And now Maddy didn't feel so alone down here anymore.

Ghosts materialized one by one. Dressed in the burial clothes from their various centuries, they walked through the walls and seeped in under the windows.

As each appeared, the ghost spoke his or her name clearly.

"Nita Naldi." From a woman in an ermine-trimmed dress with sweeping, caterpillar eyebrows.

"General Frances J. Herron." The mustached man was dressed in Union Army splendor.

"Ignatius Lupo. Call me Lupo the Wolf." This man wore high-waisted flannel slacks and had a face that was mean as a pit bull. He spat a wad of ghostly chew on the floor.

"Giulio Risseto." The boy's voice was clear as his eyes. As he became visible, he smiled at Maddy. "You used my tombstone recently to reset your shoulder. How is it?"

"Almost healed," she told him. "Thanks."

"Lucas Underhill. Call me Dad." As Dakota's dad strode out of the mist, Maddy could hear the faint clank of his foot, eternally stuck in a paint bucket. Otherwise, he looked battle ready.

"Dad!" Dakota hopped with excitement.

"Mr. Underhill's a special visitation. The rest of us are here compliments of our final resting place, the Queens Calvary Cemetery," General Herron announced with a crisp salute and a tap of his heels for Dakota's dad.

"We're glad you all came, because we need your help." Dakota's father quickly explained the situation. "We've got to haunt out the humans."

"Haunt?" Nita Naldi looked nervous. "I thought we'd been contacted to provide companionship for a lonely dryad. I've never been much for a haunting."

Maddy was upset. "There's got to be at least a million ghosts in the Calvary Cemetery. Why don't you go exchange yourselves for some spirits who like to haunt?"

General Herron looked offended. "Well, we're here now. We'll have to do."

"*I'm* ready to haunt." Lupo cracked his ghostly knuckles.

"It's just . . . most ghosts tend to be scared of Knaves," added Giulio.

"So that means you can't do anything about Zelda?" Maddy's voice wobbled in despair. "We Livingstones moved all the way here to the New World so that we didn't have to be eternal anymore. Now my poor sis is on her way to suffering one thousand years of Knav-ish immortality. In September, Lex should be starting high school. She's been looking forward to high school for almost four hundred years."

The General looked limp. "We'll give it our best."

"Okay, first things first. We don't know what we can or can't do until we get out of this dungeon," reminded Dakota.

Dakota's father extracted a large white handkerchief from his jeans pocket. "Okay, everyone ready? Follow me."

With Maddy and the others on his heel, he flowed up the cellar steps. They watched as he dissolved through the door.

He then pushed the handkerchief back underneath the space at the bottom of the door, with the key resting on top.

"Cool trick." Maddy snatched it up.

"Spirits, ready yourselves!" commanded General Herron.

Phantom arms! Just like the poem, thought Maddy as she slid the key into the lock.

19

LULLABY SHOWDOWN

Hybrids and ghosts streamed from the cellar into the ballroom.

"This place is dead. I seen better parties in my prison cell block," declared Lupo.

"And the music—so out-of-date," agreed Nita.

"That reminds me." Hudson nudged Maddy. "Remember Princess Zellandine's sweet sixteen at the Château D'Usee in Villandry, Old World?"

"Sure." A few hundred years ago, birthday girl Zellandine had pricked her finger on a spinning wheel's needle, prompting a curse that caused all the mortals to fall asleep. Only Lexie, Maddy, Hudson, and Carabosse—the thirteenth godmother—had been immune to the spell. A birthday party of sleeping guests had not been much fun, but at least there'd been plenty of cake.

"A sleep spell's what we need here," Hudson noted. "Some way to clear the humans out of the action."

"That's where we come in," said Giulio. "You go deal with your Knave. We'll take care of the rest."

He and the three other ghosts glided onto the ballroom floor, where they began to tip and sway with the dancers.

The humans were instantly befuddled. "Did someone step on my toe?" "Who just blew in my ear?"

"Oh, of course!" Hudson whispered. "The humans can't see the ghosts."

"Brr! It's cold!" the women complained as they pulled tighter on their wraps.

Creeping over to the orchestra pit, Dakota's father blew the music sheets so they scattered. Musicians looked around, frightened and confused, as the music broke off awkwardly.

"My dad's a seasoned haunter," Dakota said approvingly. "He's got the gift."

"Well, I'm a seasoned slayer," said Maddy, "and now it's time to challenge our Knave." She picked up a small drinks tray. "Try to blend in."

They inched, unseen, toward the back of the ballroom, where the Elcris family, along with Lexie and Zelda, was watching the raffle in progress while drinking from crystal goblets.

"Eeyucchh, I bet that's not wine. They're drinking rat-blood gazpacho." Dakota scrunched her face.

"I can't tell one girl from the other." Maddy's eyes darted from Zelda to Lexie and back again. Heart pounding, she approached the table. If this didn't work, all would be lost. *"Fed fest, hva?"* she asked the twins.

"Hva," replied one of the green-eyed twins, nodding.

"Da ty'de kæmper til dit skød; thi med ham lynte skræk og død," said Maddy.

"Fra vallen hørtes vrål, som brød den tykke sky," answered the other twin.

Quickly, Maddy served the glasses of water, gave a slight bow, and returned to the others. "Lexie's the one on the left," she whispered.

"How do you know?" squeaked Dakota.

"Because Zelda only learned phrase book Danish. Lexie, on the other hand, knows doomed poet Danish. Her favorite poem, 'The Death of Balder,' is by Johannes Ewald. I spoke a meter of one of his best lyrics, and she jumped right in—she couldn't help herself." But Maddy's triumph faded in a pinch as the twins jumped up from the table and moved to the dance floor, where they grasped hands and started to spin each other around and around.

"Ooh!" Dakota's eyes widened. "Now Lexie's on the right. No, the left! No, the right!"

"The Knave did it on purpose." Hudson looked sick. "They've mixed themselves up again. Now what?"

Maddy's fingers worried the beads of the von Krik necklace, as she drew it from her pocket. "Fear not, my dear Crudson," she whispered, although she knew she was betting her last trick. She waited until the dancing was over and the twins had collapsed back into their seats before she reloaded her tray with glasses of ice water. "All that exercise must have made you thirsty," she murmured as she pulled Nicola von Krik's necklace out of her pocket. "Here—from an admirer."

Both twins made a swipe for the necklace, and both

caught it by their spindly fingers. Their green eyes glittered greedily.

"For me?" asked one.

"For me?" asked the other.

"Why don't you each try it on and decide who wears it best?" Maddy suggested, then smoothly slipped away to join the others before the twins could refocus their concentration.

"Me first!" cawed a twin. Maddy, Hudson, and Dakota watched as she clasped the necklace around her throat. Instantly, the beads muddied to black.

"Now me!" The other twin snatched it off and reclasped it around her own throat. The beads mutated to a rainbow of pinks, greens, and blues.

"No, no!" Zelda shrieked. "Take that off!"

"Why? Are you jealous?" cackled the twin Maddy now knew to be her sister.

"Mads, what's going on?" Hudson hissed. "The colors are so bright. Almost unreal!"

"I think the colors of the beads reflect the blood of the wearer." Maddy blinked. She saw so little Old World magic these days that its beauty astonished her. And to think she had nearly traded that necklace away. "The beads don't know what to do with Lexie, because she's a shifter," Maddy said. "As long as it stays around her neck, Lexie can't be transformed. Like the poem says, *Glass-eyed ring should freeze this spell / Restore X from an outer shell.* If she's frozen in the spell, then she can't—" But it was

Hudson's face that had frozen as he stared at something just past Maddy's shoulder. She turned.

Zelda towered behind her, teeth bared to show her fangs, yellow as cheese and hard as steel. "I should have slayed you in the cemetery," she hissed, pointing a menacing finger so that it grazed Maddy's nose.

"Ninth Knave, relinquish my sister," Maddy snarled back.

"Not a chance, you beastly hybrid."

"Don't you know it's rude to point?" Quickly, Maddy drew the guitar pick from her pocket and sliced Zelda's fingertip.

"Ahhh!" Zelda jumped away as she licked the black blood that welled up at the cut. In the next moment, she'd recovered, and with some Old World mutterings plus a snap of her bloody fingers, she had transformed the Elcris family into four seething rats—though still very Elcris-ish. One sniffed nervously, one was bald, one had extra-beady eyes, and one had a freckly nose. They made a clawing, tail-twitching circle around Zelda, guarding her.

"Eee! Rats!" screamed a woman.

"Rats *and* ghosts! This dance is officially awful. I'm outta here!" cried the music conductor, throwing down his baton. A human stampede beat it out of the ballroom.

"Ghosts, stay put!" commanded General Herron.

"Some trick, Zelda." Maddy sneered. "It's easy to transform the Elcrises. They were so ratty already, with all that gazpacho you were feeding them. I've got the Old World recipe book, too, you know."

For the first time, Zelda lost the smug look on her face.

"Ghosts, charge the rats!" cried General Herron.

Each ghost now swooshed on the snarling rat pack. The fight was on—and the biting began. Ghosts bit rats and rats noshed ghosts.

"O dastardly dance! Please let the ghosts win," wailed Hudson, "or we are so doomed."

It didn't look good. Lupo the Wolf was first to retreat, after a hard bite on his vaporous arm. "Knave-pack rats? No, thanks. I know when I'm outmatched!" he yelped, and sprinted off.

"Rats give me the willies," fretted Nita, turning on her heel. The general followed, and they whisked away hand in hand.

"Don't leave," cried Giulio just as the freckle-nosed rat charged in with a bite on the elbow that made him yelp in pain.

Rat-Adam grinned. "Ghosts down. Hybrids next."

Giulio bounced back with a ghostly bite into Adam's tail. "Yowch!" Adam jumped back as Giulio rushed off in the opposite direction, and now Dakota's dad was the only ghost left.

Maddy gulped. One ghost, a dryad-girl, and a couple of other hybrids against four rats and a Knave. The odds weren't good.

Loud as a crack of thunder, the glass door shattered into a blizzard of shards as the beast leaped through.

"A dingo!" shrieked Dakota.

The rats cowered as the beast crouched, his breath heaving, his claws digging welts into the slippery ballroom floor.

Maddy hauled up the didgeridoo like a baseball bat. "What Knavish monster are you?" she called. "Prepare for combat!"

"No, Maddy," Hudson murmured. "Put down the didge, and look into his eyes."

But the wolf's eyes now had targeted Zelda, who let out a terrifying cry. In the next second, she'd morphed into a black rat and was racing for the window. Quickly, Dakota's dad stuck out his paint-bucketed foot, tripping and flipping the rat over on her back. And now the wolf lunged, his lips drawn back over his gums, to tear a bloody bite into Zelda the rat's side.

"Ahhh!" Screeching, Zelda flipped back onto her feet to transform once more, into a Knaveheart vampire bat. Wings unfurling, fangs like knives as she exploded into her full strength. She shot up to the roof's rafter, then honed in on the wolf, bearing down on him like a bullet.

Maddy acted quick. She blew as hard as she could into the didge, blasting the noise straight into the Knaveheart's extra-sensitive bat ear. Shocked, Zelda veered and dipped low.

Once again, the wolf leaped.

Maddy covered her ears as she heard the sickening rip of bat wing. With a strangled cry, the Knaveheart flew out the window.

"She won't get far," muttered Hudson. "A bat is not uni-wingular."

Dakota gagged at the bloodied scrap of wing that had splatted onto her foot. "Get it off!"

Brave Maddy picked it off and flung it to the side.

"Thanks." Dakota sagged with relief.

"That's what friends are for," said Maddy.

They all ran to the window and watched as the bat began to list before she dropped into the holly hedges. They heard a soft plop and a sizzling noise followed by a scorched odor, like burning bacon—the most anti-vegan smell in the odor spectrum.

"Ugh." Maddy pinched her nose.

As the smell drifted into the ballroom, Lexie exhaled long and deep as the trance released. Everyone stared as her ears sprang back through her now iron-straight hair and her nose took on its usual pointy pinch. Her dress became baggier and baggier as she slowly shrank to her previous Lexie size.

Maddy watched in wonder as her sister's gaze, sharp and dark once more, found the wolf. She flew across the room and threw her arms around his neck.

"You!" she cried, burying her face in his neck ruff. "You wonderful wolf! Thank you, Pete!"

Pete the wolf licked her face sloppily.

By this time, a few brave humans had straggled back to the ballroom, only to find a wolf in their midst. Again they screamed and scrambled. "Wolf! Wolf! Somebody kill him!"

"I'll handle this." Mr. Elcris, reshaped into human form, grabbed for a pair of ice tongs and charged the wolf.

But he was too slow and no match besides. His work complete, Pete had already leaped through the broken doors and back into the night.

20

RUNNING WATER

Of course you *all* saved me," said Lexie as she sprinkled paprika on her famous shredded carrot salad.

"But you have to agree, *my* save was the most dramatic," added Pete. "It's part of the deal when you're a werewolf."

"True. Everyone loves a good swashbuckling rescue." Lexie's voice was too goopy, in Maddy's opinion, and her eyes too dewy as she let Pete test the salad but then swatted Hudson's hand away.

It was exactly one week later, and the Livingstones were celebrating the release of their parents' new album by hosting a lunch party. Everyone had been invited, and it wasn't long before the dining room table was crowded with Dead Ringers band members, Wander Wag dog walkers, Candlewick Café staff, and a handful of ghosts from the Calvary Cemetery. Though none of the mortals could see the phantoms, it was a good party mix. Even Dakota and her parents were here, as well as Carlyle Blake, dapper as ever in a lemonade yellow linen suit.

Lisi had showed up, too, with Adam. They were a last-minute suggestion from Dakota. "Please invite her, Maddy? She really wants to become friendly with you,"

Dakota had pleaded. "She feels bad about the whole Knave thing. She hadn't realized that her cousin from Denmark was so dangerous—and flammable."

"No way! Lisi Elcris is a scab on top of a bruise."

"Please? I'll let you use my didge." So then Maddy didn't really have a choice.

When Lisi showed up on the Livingstone doorstep, she'd presented Maddy with an Elcris Shoe Emporium shoe box. "For you!"

Maddy mistrusted the little smile on Lisi's face. Could it possibly be a Box of Disgusting? Was Lisi on to Maddy's best trick? But when Maddy opened the shoe box top at arm's length, guarding herself from what might be inside, all she found were her dear old sneakers.

"They were in Lullaby's lost and found," said Lisi. "I saw your initials on the bottom in purple Magic Marker. I figured you might want 'em back." She shrugged. "People get attached to their sneaks."

"Hey, thanks." Maddy slipped them on. Maybe Lisi wasn't all bad. Maybe she'd even be a good candidate for helping Maddy to create future Boxes of Disgusting. After all, those Elcris shoe boxes were everywhere.

"By the way, your sister's sneakers stink," added Adam to Hudson. "She should come down to Elcris Shoe Emporium for a new pair."

"Finally, an original thought. Keep 'em coming, squirt." Hudson slapped Adam on the back as he led them all to the dining room. "Lunch is this way. Buffet style."

When Orville showed up a little later, in human form

as Mr. Schnur, he tipped a ghostly Lupo the Wolf off his chair and promptly seated himself and his full plate next to Maddy. Ugh. Now she couldn't gulp the drowsy house-fly that had been buzzing around the fruit bowl center-piece.

Orville must have noticed her hungry eyes on the insect. "Good job releasing your sister from that Knave, Maddy. But don't lose sight of the reason why you came to the New World. If you want to be mortal, you must banish your vestigial vampire traits. Like bloodthirst."

Maddy nodded, but when Orville wasn't looking, she caught the fly with her tongue, sucked out the blood, then spit the buggy leftovers into her napkin. After all, she was a slayer of purebloods and a Knave hunter. And right now she wasn't sure she was ready to give up those titles in the name of plain old vanilla mortality.

After lunch, Carlyle asked the band to play one of their songs. "I prefer opera, but I do want to hear something modern—if it's not too tedious."

Dakota's dad picked up his clarinet. "I'll play along."

"Wonderful!" said their mother, though the mortals all looked at her strangely, since she seemed to be speaking to a mirror propped against an empty chair.

Maddy herself could only see the faintest outline of Dakota's dad, but she could find him easily in the music that wafted through the air, audible to all, as he played a scale and then accompanied the Dead Ringers through a few of their new tunes.

"Hex, you should give Dakota's dad that clarinet,"

Maddy suggested to her sister. "Especially now that you've decided to take up . . ." She tried not to roll her eyes. "The harp."

"Ooh, that reminds me." Lexie jumped up and ran off, returning with her newest instrument. She plucked a few notes. "I just learned a very tragic song called 'Running Water.' Wanna hear?"

"Of course, darling," chorused her parents.

"Not really," said Maddy.

"Supportive!" Pete reminded as Lexie tuned up.

"'Once victim, always victim,'" Maddy quoted back. "That's what Lexie says when the same horrible thing happens over and over. For example, like Lexie continuing to believe that she's musically gifted."

On her one side, Dakota giggled.

On her other side, Lisi passed the huckleberry pie. "Get some before Adam goes for thirds. If he eats any more, he might turn into a huckleberry himself."

"Thanks." As Maddy took a slice, she realized—here she was, at the end of the summer, sitting between her two friends. Real friends, not imaginary ones. And not just for a day, since Dakota and Lisi had decided Maddy's bedroom was gruesome enough for a spooky haunted house sleepover. (Whatever that meant. So far, all the ghosts Maddy knew were pretty tame.)

But no friend could have replaced her sister. Maddy's eyes itched to think about how close she'd been to losing Lex. Even now, the von Krik necklace that sparkled around Lexie's throat was a reminder that she needed protection against shifting under a stronger vampire's influence. Thankfully, Carlyle had agreed to let Maddy trade it back for Hudson's vintage Russian costume. Of course, Crud still didn't know about that.

"Running water, running water. Where are you running from?" sang Lexie in her fruity, not-that-good voice. "You always seem to be on the run."

And the guests and ghosts all nodded along, in the spirit of the tune.

MADDY'S
STRENGTH DOUBLER
A Guaranteed Energy Boost for Vampires,
*Humans, and Horses**

In a juicer add:
1 large, violet beet
1 parsnip
$\frac{1}{2}$ bitter turnip
$\frac{1}{2}$ cup cranberries
1 whole cup blueberries
1 bunch kale
1 bunch bok choy
1 red cabbage
2 large celery stalks
3 rutabagas

After these vegetables and fruits have been juiced, pour the juice in a blender and add:

2 tbsp. powdered vitamins
2 tbsp. wheat germ
1 tbsp. gelatin
1 tsp. cod liver oil
1 tsp. cinnamon for flavor
1 tsp. Tabasco sauce for kick**

Transfer into a bowl. Refrigerate overnight. Delicious! Double your energy!

*If planning to feed this to a horse,
substitute wheat germ with carrots or apples.*
**Desiccated moth wings not recommended.*

$\mathcal{L}$exie's
LATEST LIST OF THE BRILLIANT
AND (OCCASIONALLY) DOOMED

Elizabeth Bishop (1911–1979) *"The art of losing isn't hard to master; so many things seem filled with the intent / to be lost that their loss is no disaster."*

Jeff Buckley (1966–1997) *"This is our last goodbye / I hate to feel the love between us die / But it's over / Just hear this and then I'll go / You gave me more to live for than you'll ever know."*

Tess Durbeyfield / *Tess of the D'Urbervilles*, by Thomas Hardy (1840–1928) *"Once victim, always victim—that's the law!"*

Johannes Ewald (1743–1781) *"Then champions to thine arms were sent / Terror and Death glared where he went / From the waves was heard a wail that rent / Thy murky sky!"*

Billie Holiday (1915–1959) *"Life's dreary for me / Days seem to be long as years / I've looked for the sun / But can see none / Through my tears."*

Daniel Johnston (1961–) *"Running water / Running water / Where are you running from? / You always seem to be on the run!"*

Elliott Smith (1969–2003) *"Do you miss me miss misery / Like you say you do?"*

Timid Frieda / "Timid Frieda," by Jacques Brel (1929–1978) *"Timid Frieda, If you see her / On the street where the future gathers / Just let her be her, let her play in / The broken times of sand."*

Dr. Yuri Zhivago / Dr. Zhivago, by Boris Pasternak (1890–1960) *"The more we love, the more the object of our love seems to be a victim."*

Hudson Livingstone's
Book Report

VLAD THE IMPALER AND DANIEL BOONE:
A COMPARATIVE BIOGRAPHY

Wilderness explorer Daniel Boone was born in 1734, near Reading, Pennsylvania, many centuries after, and on an entirely different continent from, nobleman Vlad Tepes, who was born in 1431 in a high fortress overlooking Sighisoara, Romania, Old World.

As a lad, Daniel Boone befriended Native New Worlders. He enjoyed learning the ways and habits of wild animals, though he was just as quick to kill them with his spears. Young Boone soon became a rifle-carrying huntsman. In contrast, young Vlad soon learned the ways and habits of angry mobs when his brother was blinded by warring Turks, who stuck hot pokers into his eyes before they buried him alive.

After Boone served in the French and Indian War, he returned home to marry his beloved, Rebecca Bryan. Together they built a modest homestead. Vengeful longtime bachelor Vlad never stopped fighting the Turks, and eventually he and his army took over Hungaria. Once Vlad had established leadership, he conscripted a thousand of his slaves to build the fearsome Castle Dracul. After the slaves' hard work, Vlad ordered them all to be impaled, and he displayed their heads on his spiked gates.

A dedicated explorer, Daniel Boone had plenty of friends

and shared adventures with them. He and his comrades explored Kentucky all the way to the Falls of the Ohio. On another trip, Boone tracked the Kentucky River to its mouth. A dedicated tyrant, Vlad's army terrorized and pillaged whenever they got the chance. He loved conquering new land, and he took pleasure in causing misery to his foes through torture. Among his gruesome means of murder: boiling, beheading, scalping, hanging, and, of course, burying alive.

Boone left the Bluegrass in 1788, moving into uncharted West Virginia. Many years later, he decided to explore the Missouri region. Lore has it that as he paddled his canoe downriver, somebody asked him why he was leaving Kentucky. "Too crowded!" quipped the prospector. Vlad's exploits also earned him a nickname, "Dracula," meaning "Son of the Dragon." Stories of his reign became legend. But all horrifying eras must end, and eventually Vlad was driven from power.

Boone died peacefully at the age of eighty-five. He was buried beside his wife in Missouri. Twenty-five years later, the couple's bodies were brought back to the Bluegrass and laid to rest in Frankfort Cemetery, where you can visit their graves today. Vlad's last chapter was not so lucky. Without a throne or any more peasants to kill, his hunger for blood caused him to go insane. He was assassinated in 1476, and his corpse was decapitated by one of his many enemies. Nobody knows exactly where this dreadful Knaveheart is buried, and his coffin has never been found.

ADELE GRIFFIN is the critically acclaimed author of numerous novels for young adults, including *Vampire Island* and National Book Award Finalists *Where I Want to Be* and *Sons of Liberty*. She lives in Brooklyn, New York.

Visit Adele Griffin at **www.adelegriffin.net**.

Learn more about the world of Vampire Island at
http://bite-me-blog.blogspot.com/
and
www.myspace.com/vladandlexie

IN NEED OF A FRIEND...

Maddy Livingstone is a fruit-bat vampire hybrid with no social graces—which doesn't exactly make her popular with other eleven-year-olds. But when the leader of the Knavehearts—the most vicious of the Old World vampires—comes to town, Maddy befriends Dakota Underhill. Maddy's not strong enough to face the villain alone, and there's something special about Dakota that might make her the perfect person to team up with....

"Griffin whips humor, suspense and frequent, offhand gross bits into a winning formula that young readers will slurp up avidly." —*Kirkus Reviews*

SCHOLASTIC
www.scholastic.com

ISBN: 978-0-545-22393-5
EAN
9 780545 223935